# SAWYER

The Gates – Book 7

**M. Tasia**

2

# ALSO BY M. TASIA

## The Boys of Brighton series
*Gabe*
*Sam's Soldiers*
*Rick's Bear*
*Jesse*
*Coop*
*Travis*
*Grady*
*Vincent*
*Shadow*
*The Holidays*

## The Gates series
*Saint*
*Finn*
*James*
*Joey*
*Bradley*
*Carlos*

# EVERYONE LOVES THE BOYS OF BRIGHTON

*"I loved this book and I love this town. I hope there's going to be more."*
—Melissa Lemons on *Gabe*

*"An amazing read that was filled with lust, love, crazy hot sex, danger, action and so much more This is the first book I have read in this series but I will definitely be reading more in the future."*
—Gay Book Reviews on *Sam's Soldiers*

*"I was crazy impressed that the author made me teary over the ending of a relationship that I shouldn't have even been invested in. I didn't yet know these characters yet the author made me hurt for them. That takes some mad writing skills!"*
—Love Bytes Reviews

*"Jesse and Royce together have my heart. Jesse has it all by himself."*
—The Book Junkie Reads on *Jesse*

*"So much action, intrigue, drama and angst for the long awaited story of Grady and Ben. This was worth the wait. Sexy and sweet. I can't wait for the next."*
—SamD on *Grady*

*"I knew this one would be my favorite to date! There was something about Vincent that said awesome then came Tristan."*
—Booky on *Vincent*

*"This installment of the Boys of Brighton was so good! I loved Shadow and Randy 's story I was hooked from the first page to the last. This book was definitely worth the wait!"*
—AG on *Shadow*

*"I have loved this series from the very first story and this holiday novella is simply perfect. We get a glimpse of all our couples and what is happening in their lives while the holidays explode around them. I cannot wait for more!"*

—bookobsessed on *The Holidays*

# EVERYONE'S NEWEST LOVE – THE GATES

*"Having read the entire Boys of Brighton series, I was eagerly awaiting Saint's story and it was so worth the wait. I enjoyed every word. I am always amazed by authors that bring characters to life so much that you can hardly wait for the next story. Cannot wait for Finn and Miguel to have their turn. While I'm waiting I'll reread the Boys of Brighton series!"*
—Debbie Kay on *Saint*

*"Ms. Tasia has done it again! This is Saint's story, for readers of the Brighton Boys, you'll know he needs a break! After being forced to become a plastic surgeon by his father, he rebels by assisting people in 3rd world countries, which puts him in the position to be kidnapped and tortured. You really feel for him, that's for sure! Max is the perfect man for poor Saint's battered soul, not that he doesn't have his own issues! Overall, this was engaging, steady paced and chock full of all the feels!"*
—Avid Reader on *Saint*

*"Finn and Miguel stole my heart. This is a great Sunday afternoon read. Finn's character jumped off the page as his story developed through each chapter. I loved reading his truth and watching him and Miguel find their home in each other."*
—K.A. Brown on *Finn*

*"Another tale from the Gates of Heaven, another two brilliant MCs we get to know very well. I loved both the plot and the characters, all their emotions and insecurities on full display. All the descriptions and world building were very vivid, providing a great background for an emotional story of self discovery and developing attraction."*
—AL on *Finn*

*"James...what can I say. I couldn't put it down. This is my first book in the series, so it definitely can be read and enjoyed as a*

*standalone, but it will not be my last. Now I'm going to read the previous stories. Solid writing with a gripping style, characters that are right up my alley, and the kind of chemistry I love in my romances. What more do you need for a great reading experience."*
—cinnamon on *James*

*"This is really a great series and I def recommend it. I loved James and Ross, it was a rough start for the two, but they worked it out. I can't wait for more, love everything M. TASIA writes!"*
—TammyKay on *James*

*"I may have my new favorite book couple of the series. Joey and Sam just have that something special. At one point I was ugly crying but it was a good ugly cry if that makes any sense. I really love the series and I can't wait for her next installment!!"*
—Vine Voice on *Joey*

*"M. Tasia is an automatic 1 click author for me...she definitely didn't disappoint with Joey."*
—Heather Weissman on *Joey*

*"This author is really talented and I love her series, this one and the Boys of Brighton. Her characters are so well drawn and I can really get into the stories. I especially loved Eric in this particular book. I'm hoping Clay the rookie will be the next book. Keep 'em coming!"*
—Rosemary on *Bradley*

*"All the stories in this series have their own brand of excitement, this being no exception. All previous books include former heroes from the series which I find very charming. Our heroes here, Eric and Brad, give us another great performance. A villain surfaces and wreaks havoc on the lives of good people and is, after a stretch, put in his place. The book is a love story with a dose of excitement and, unfortunately, a bit of homophobia thrown in. A story nicely told."*
—Tappy on *Bradley*

*"Accompanying the gentle blooming of love between the damaged men, is gorgeous description. M. Tasia captivated me with her vivid*

*illustrations of scenery and tourist sites (I feel as if I've explored CA and AZ beside the leading men), mouthwatering food, and intriguing art. I found myself wondering, is M. Tasia so well-traveled? A foodie? An art connoisseur? Or did she simply do her author's research very well?*

*Carlos is a tender romance coupled with mystery and suspense, not to mention several surprises at the end. In M. Tasia's words, "rebirth and determination" are a profound theme of the story, relating to people and places. This is a moving read, and a quickly devoured one, too, as it's difficult to put down."*
—Kristen A. Remick on *Carlos*

*"Carlos is ready to come out of seclusion. He wants to live near his brother, Miguel, experience the world outside his doors, allow the world to enhance his art. It's this brother who brings Clay into his life, a cop who quickly becomes Carlos' everything.*

*Two men with damaged souls come together and find love. A tried and true formula that works well here, especially when working with two lovable characters like Carlos and Clay. Carlos especially was interesting to me - the contrast of his appearance to his gentle nature, a true gentle giant. And Clay being all protective of the much larger, but more gentle man - so sweet! I really liked this story and am looking forward to more of The Gates now."*
—Valeen on *Carlos*

www.BOROUGHSPUBLISHINGGROUP.com

SAWYER
Copyright © 2021 M. Tasia

ISBN: 978-1-953810-29-8

*This has been possible because of the love and support of my family. Love you Craig, Samantha, Katie, and Jason.*

# ACKNOWLEDGMENTS

Thank you to my amazing publisher for taking the time to play tour guide in her diverse and stunning area of Southern California. Your indomitable spirit and strength inspires me to continue to grow as an author. Also, to my sisters-in-law, thank you for coming along and supporting my dream. The love and strength of family is the cornerstone of my career.

# SAWYER

# Chapter One

Sawyer pulled another rack of steaming plates and silverware from the industrial dishwasher's conveyor belt that ran along the kitchen's back wall at The Gates. He carried it over to one of the two stacking tables before returning to put a rack of dirty wine glasses through. He hoped he had time to get to the pots and pans, which were soaking in hot, soapy water in the extra-large stainless-steel sinks a few feet away.

It'd been another busy night in the restaurant, which meant a steady stream of dirty dishes from the moment he came on shift. He didn't mind. Work was work, and it made the evening go by faster. Not that quick passage of time was a boon.

Once the wine glasses were in the dishwasher, he turned his attention to collecting the full dish bins from the wait staff area behind the restaurant. He was careful to look through the window of the kitchen's swinging doors before opening the right side. Last week he hadn't, and a waiter with a full tray of desserts was walking by, and everything the dude was carrying wound up on the floor. The head chef had torn a strip off him.

Sawyer looked both ways and slowly opened the door. The coast was clear. He stepped out into the fray and felt like he was playing that old video game where you tried to get your frog to the other side of the road without being hit by a car. He dodged a guy carrying six plates on a large round tray and wondered how the wait staff balanced so much food in one trip. Food would be hanging from the chandeliers if he tried that.

Quickly, he picked up a full tub of dirty dishes, turned to take them into the back of the house, and was cut off by a busboy heading in the opposite direction. The sudden stop shifted his leg brace, causing him to misstep, and before he knew what was happening, he was falling face forward to the tiled floor. He closed his eyes, and at the last moment, a strong hand grabbed him under his arm, stopping his fall at the same time taking hold of the dish bin with the other hand.

Sawyer regained his footing and looked up to find the last person he ever wanted to screw-up in front of: the award-winning renowned head chef, Alexander Larsen. Sawyer's heart sank. He'd been working at The Gates for seven months and liked it here. He didn't want to be fired. Even though Marian ran the kitchen, Sawyer was sure one bad word from Alexander, and boom, Sawyer would be out.

"I'm sorry," he sputtered. "It won't happen again." He'd re-adjust his brace out back.

"You okay?" Alexander asked with what sounded like actual concern.

"Uh... I'm fine, sir."

"Alexander, not sir," he ordered.

"Yes, Alexander, sir."

When Alexander looked like he was about to say something else, a waitress cleared her throat to get the chef's attention. "Table seven is waiting, Chef."

Sawyer turned his head to see a few people had stopped to stare. A couple of times a night, guests would request to meet the chef to heap on accolades, which explained why Alexander was outside of his kitchen fiefdom.

Sawyer adjusted his leg and took a better hold of the dish tub. "Thank you for your help."

Slowly, Alexander released him before nodding his head and followed the waitress into the restaurant. Sawyer limped to the wash area, set down the tub on the sorting table, and quickly readjusted and tightened his right leg brace. He knew his constant remedial repairs would eventually fail, but a new brace didn't come cheap. He'd stretch the life out of this one for as long as he could.

Sawyer kept his head down, fearing the guillotine could be triggered at any moment, and his job would be taken away. It wasn't as if this had been his career path. Far from it, but he had to do what he must to get by.

The sick feeling in his stomach intensified as the night wore on. As the clock neared ten, the rush of dishes slowed as the restaurant prepared to close. The front lounge remained open until midnight for drinks only. He removed his last rack of dishes from the machine and tidied his area before Marian came out to inspect the kitchen before shutting it down until tomorrow morning. With its late work hours, this job was perfect since he was pretty tied up during the day.

"I see you're ready to go home."

He jumped at the voice not typically heard in the wash area. "Yes, sir. I mean, Alexander." *What the fuck is he doing back here?*

"How's your leg?" The tall, brooding man asked, looking down at Sawyer's brace.

"Fine, strong as ever." It wasn't an out and out lie. His right leg was as strong as ever, which meant it was typically weak and sore. However, Chef didn't need to know that.

Marian walked in and took a long look at the two of them. "There a problem?"

This was it. His time here was over. They didn't need a clumsy dishwasher breaking place settings and costing them money. Damn, at twenty-six, he'd hoped he'd have life figured out, but here he was, desperately trying to hold onto a dishwasher position.

"No. No problem," Alexander answered Marian, but kept looking at Sawyer. "I was checking on Sawyer's leg."

How did Alexander know his name? Sawyer was about as far away from the kitchen as anyone could get in the back of the restaurant.

"Something's wrong with your leg?" Marian came closer with furrowed brows.

"No. A Velcro strap loosened, making me misstep. It's tightened now."

"Good. As long as you're okay." Marian gave him a shrewd look before handing him a paper bag. "I noticed you didn't stop for lunch again. Free food is part of working here. I made you a to-go bag."

"Thank you." Sawyer reached for a bag that was much heavier than a mere sandwich. "Have a good night."

He went to the employee lounge adjacent to the kitchen to get his jacket and backpack. Without looking at what Marian had put in the paper bag, he stuffed it into his backpack, shrugged into his jacket, and headed for the door to walk home as he did every night.

He knew walking in some areas of DTLA late at night was risky, but he knew the neighborhoods like the back of his hand. He'd grown up among these people and played in streets that would scare most suburban folks to death.

The flickering streetlights and dark alleyways welcomed him as he walked down the back steps of The Gates. He called the creatures of the night by name, having lived side by side with them since birth. The corner dealers, the gangs that marked their territory, along with the hustlers, the thieves, the sex workers, and their clients, all of whom walked the same sidewalks as he did.

He didn't fear nighttime in the city. He feared the light of day when the bureaucrats returned to their offices in the tall, steel buildings to screw with other people's lives. The same people who were behind the stacks of court papers littering his dining room table.

A whistle caught his attention, and he turned to look and saw Miss Chiffon, a local sex worker, headed his way. He didn't know if she was named after the cloth or the cake. Her hair was done up in a bouffant over three inches high, and her makeup was perfect. She worked a skintight leopard-print dress and swished in those stiletto heels she loved so much. He never could figure out how women walked in those things. She cut a striking figure, and Sawyer was sure the middle-aged woman attracted her share of men.

She wasn't his type, and they both knew it.

"Hey, Miss Chiffon. How are you this evening?" He waited for her to catch up.

She came to stand beside him while pulling a sleek, black compact from her red, fake alligator bag and used a puff to dab her nose. He didn't see the need and gave a mental shrug. Women "fixed" their faces all the time.

"Bored, Sawyer," she groaned. "There's nothing happening tonight. I can't even scare up a blowjob."

"Don't look at me." Sawyer laughed. "I'm fine."

"The day you take me up on an offer, I'll be looking to the skies," she said while lifting her arms dramatically toward the heavens.

"The skies?"

"Yep," she said. "Flying pigs would leave considerably more shit behind than any bird ever could when flying over you."

Sawyer couldn't help but laugh. The woman was all glitz and glamor on the outside, but the real Miss Chiffon came out when she spoke. A dramatic, beautiful, foul-mouthed, opinionated woman who he'd come to love over the years. They walked for another block, with Miss Chiffon adjusting her pace to match his, which he appreciated considering he didn't have the energy to try to keep up with her tonight.

"Sweetie, you look exhausted, and not in a good, just-got-your-rocks-off, way."

"Busy night at work," he said. "Surprised I didn't get fired. It was a hell of a night."

"Fired. Who would fire you? You're one of the hardest working people I know."

"I'm also clumsy," he sighed. "One of the straps on my leg brace keeps coming loose, and I almost dropped an entire bin of plates."

"Almost?"

"Yeah. The head chef, Alexander, saved me." Sawyer shook his head. "He caught me before I hit the ground."

"Alexander, huh? You've mentioned him before," she said as her smile widened. "Mr. tall, dark, and hopefully well-endowed for your sake."

"Yeah, I'm sure a Michelin Star chef wants to hang out with the dishwasher on the regular. Besides, that's the last thing I need right now." As if he didn't have enough shit on his plate.

Her expression turned concerned. "How's Bobby?"

"Same as yesterday and the day before. I keep expecting him to snap out of it, but I guess the professionals were right." Even though he was loath to admit it.

"Fuck the professionals. Excuse my French," she said while fluffing her shiny black hair. Miss Chiffon spoke fluent, "French."

"The way I see it," she continued, "they sit in their offices lording over us like we should be thankful for them. They have the power and seldom use it for good."

Sawyer agreed wholeheartedly. In his experience, a suit and tie came with a flashing warning sign: Stay away from the lying, scheming SOB.

"I'm not locking Bobby away. Fuck them."

"Damn straight, sweetie." Miss Chiffon wove her arm through his in a show of solidarity. He adored her.

A car slowed down beside them to keep pace as they walked. Miss Chiffon's eyes brightened, and she added a bit more swing to her hips. Sawyer would never knock anyone trying to make a living, but he worried for her. Men were dangerous and unpredictable. Making him wonder why he was so attracted to them.

"Hey, sweetheart, you want a date?" a deep voice hollered from the driver's seat.

Miss Chiffon perked up even more when she heard the voice. "Is that you, Robert? You old dog, when did you get back in town?" She stopped walking and approached the 80's vintage Lincoln Continental.

"Yesterday, doll. Hop in. Have you eaten yet today?"

By now, Sawyer was a few feet away, so she blew him a kiss. "Talk later, sweetie."

"Good night, Miss Chiffon." He waved, comforted that this guy was a regular of hers, making it relatively safer than a nobody."

After two more blocks, he walked up to his building. It wasn't run down but like many buildings in DTLA, old with faded awnings and chipped bricks. Without the life insurance payments, there'd be no chance he'd be able to afford living here even though it was necessary. This was the same building he'd grown up in, though in a different apartment than he had now. The hallways were clean, and the super was decent. What more could he ask for?

Sawyer pushed the cracked button for the third floor and waited for the elevator doors to open, releasing him. His apartment wasn't far, which he appreciated right about now, given how bad his leg was throbbing.

He unlocked his front door and dropped his backpack inside the hallway. Through the dimmed lights, he saw a lone figure lay sleeping on his couch. He made his way over and softly tapped Mrs. Garnet's right shoulder. The older woman's eyes popped open almost instantly.

"Hi," he whispered. "Thanks for watching him for me tonight."

"No problem. He was an angel. If you happen to pick up an extra shift again, I'm more than happy to help out." She stood and slowly straightened with the odd moan. "These old bones take a minute to get moving."

"So do these twenty-six-year-old bones," he teased. "Tell Mr. Garnet I'll be over tomorrow to help him with the kitchen sink."

"That'll be wonderful, dear," she said as she opened the apartment door. "Thing's been leaking for months. Good night, Sawyer."

"Good night, Mrs. Garnet." The older lady had been a godsend. The service sent Janice five days a week. The weekends were his chance to score extra shifts, and the service didn't cover weekends.

Sawyer shut and locked the door once his neighbor made it inside her apartment. He picked up his backpack and went straight to the fridge for a beer. The one pleasure he still allowed himself.

The crisp hissing sound as the can cracked open rang through his small galley kitchen. He took a swig before opening his backpack and pulling out the bag Marian had given him, setting it in the fridge to save for tomorrow because it was his day off.

Finally, he made his way to his recliner in the living room between the couch and the door. With an exhausted huff, he sat down and took another swig of his beer. The glow from the streetlights was enough to see by. He didn't bother turning on a lamp. He glanced down at his bedding tucked beside the chair and wondered if he had the energy to bother using it tonight.

He undid the straps on his leg brace and pulled his useless appendage out from the confines of the steel and fabric. It was easier for him to walk around at home without it because there were plenty of sturdy things to hold on to. His mother's china cabinet, a couch, chairs, his father's writing desk, and an old twenty-six-inch television on top of an even older wall unit.

No matter where he looked, his gaze was drawn back to the electric wheelchair sitting in the corner.

The mass of steel similar but so much bigger and more essential than his brace was for his younger brother, Bobby. Both of them were trapped in bodies that no longer worked as they should. But for Bobby, the failure was extreme. Karma or fate, possibly both, had a hand in readjusting their futures. Whichever, the bitch was not kind.

As he drifted off to sleep, he thought, *another day in paradise.*

# Chapter Two

"I can't believe I let you talk me into moving across the country," Cooper yelled as another piece of luggage was hurled out from their bedroom, landing a few feet away from where Alexander was pouring himself another scotch, neat. "The west coast sucks."

"I don't remember talking you into anything, but if that's the way you choose to remember it, fine." Alexander didn't want to argue. He wanted quiet. Peace and quiet.

"Of all the restaurants in the world, why this one? It's a nothing with a nobody owner that opened only in the last two years," he complained while Alexander sipped his drink and wondered what the hell he'd ever seen in the trust-fund brat throwing yet another tantrum. Sure, he was handsome and a good fuck, but besides that, their personalities clashed like oil and water.

Where he saw opportunity and adventure, Cooper found a dead end and wasted time. Their differences floated to the surface over the past year since Alexander accepted the executive chef position at The Gates. A day didn't go by without some sort of snide remark or jab about Alexander's career being over.

"You don't spend any time with me anymore," Cooper whined, which sounded like nails on a chalkboard. "I'm lonely."

"Building a world-class restaurant takes time and devotion, things you haven't got a clue about. Besides, you didn't look lonely with your feet in the air with your trainer." It still struck Alexander how little it truly bothered him that Cooper was cheating on him and was even now packing to head back East.

"You drove me into those arms," Cooper growled as he stormed out into the foyer to collect his bags. "What? I supposed sit in this condo day after day?"

"No one was chaining you to the building. You could've done any number of things with your time. Get a hobby, charity work, join a club, or here's a novel thought: get a job. So, get over it and get out." There was no way he'd allow Cooper to twist this around.

Cooper stood in the center of a pile of his luggage, his blond hair tussled and blue eyes staring daggers straight at Alexander. "Look at you. Standing there, drinking your scotch as if my leaving was nothing more than a formality. I'm Cooper Hitchford, asshole."

"Yes, you are," Alexander agreed before pulling his vibrating phone out of his pocket and reading the message on the screen. "And your taxi is waiting for you downstairs."

Alexander would be bet his best knife that wasn't the response Cooper had been going for. His flushed face made him look ready to explode. Sure, Cooper's family was rich, but so was Alexander's. Therefore, that name drop power play didn't quite work. Cooper wasn't taking being broken up with well for one reason only: he was used to getting everything he ever wanted.

"I'll destroy you. I'll have my father's people destroy your reputation. You'll no longer be a Michelin Star Chef, and The Gates will rue the day they offered you this position," Cooper said, and Alexander could see the wheels turning in his glare.

Okay, that made Alexander laugh. "Your family barely tolerates you. They give you money to go away. I can't see you rousing your father's support in that endeavor considering he'd asked me on numerous occasions what it was I saw in you." Cruel but true, and considering Cooper had begun with the threats, Alexander felt justified in sharing these truths. Bitchy, but satisfying.

Before Cooper could get in another word, the doorbell rang, and Alexander yelled for them to come in, considering he already knew who it would be.

The front door opened wide, revealing his doorman. "Good Evening, John. Right on time. Could you please escort Mr. Hitchford from my home?"

"Certainly, sir," John replied but didn't make a move to reach down to pick up Cooper's luggage. Instead, the large man placed his hands behind his back and did his best impersonation of a wall, which elicited another laugh from Alexander.

"I see another bridge you've burned, Cooper," he said. "Maybe it was the way you belittled the staff even after I warned you. Or it could be the time you threatened to call immigration on the employees. Who knows, but all that matters now is that you leave the key fob on your way out."

Cooper had made the immigration threat less than a week ago, and Alexander had been thinking of ways to extricate the rude, mean-spirited man from his life. In truth, the trainer couldn't have done him a bigger favor by sleeping with Alexander's ex. God, he loved that word associated with Cooper.

"You haven't heard the last of me," Cooper threatened. "You've fucked with the wrong person."

"No, actually, you were fucking the wrong person earlier when I found you. Do you think it's wise to threaten me in front of a witness? I don't believe your family would appreciate the police involvement."

That got his attention. Cooper angrily pulled out his keyring from his pocket, removed the fob, and slammed it on the entrance side table. "Fuck you."

"Never again," Alexander said cheerfully while raising his glass in salute.

John walked over and began herding Cooper and his luggage out the door. Alexander's doorman was a gift. He'd been working long hours to bring the food at The Gates to a whole new level and hadn't realized the shit disturbing his ex was doing while Alexander was at work.

Christmas bonuses would need to be doubled this year as an apology for his lapse in judgment.

Once he heard the door click shut, he sunk into his large sectional sofa and stared out at the lights coming from windows in neighboring high-rises. His stress slowly began to fade as peace reigned in his two-bedroom condo on Wilshire Boulevard.

He'd grown up in a family similar to Cooper's, but with one crucial difference: a conscience. Old family money had sat in many bank accounts earning outrageous interest in his great-grandfather and grandfather's days. However, the moment Alexander's father inherited the fortune, he went about changing the status quo.

Instead of languishing and gathering dust, Roger Larsen went about spending the money in the most outrageous of ways, at least according to his forefathers: philanthropy.

Charities received yearly endowments, which enabled wings to be added to pediatric cancer wards in honor of Alexander's brother, who died of brain cancer before reaching the age of one. Scholarships were created to help underfunded urban schools across the country, and over one-thousand students had already graduated from college programs, thanks to his father's mission.

Alexander looked up to his father and everything he'd accomplished. Careful investing kept the family flush, and allowed them to live well and continue his father's legacy. When he'd been a teenager, Alexander knew straight up the money wasn't his. His father had made that clear from the moment he could understand what a dollar was and how you used it to buy things.

Because he'd been born into the family didn't mean shit. He had to prove himself capable of handling the responsibility that came with great wealth. Conversely, the family doled out love freely. Alexander always knew he was cherished.

He'd been attending Harvard Business School when he found his passion for food and cooking. He'd been sharing an apartment with two school friends that had an ongoing competition over dinner, more specifically, who was the better cook. He'd spent that entire term eating everything from Boeuf Bourguignon and Coq au Vin to Baked Alaska and Paella. He'd gained ten pounds being the taste-tester.

When he graduated the following year, he decided to explore the culinary world, backpacking through Europe and working in restaurants along the way. He'd washed countless dishes and diced pounds of Mirepoix, fished among the families, scrubbed the floors, and cleaned more toilets than he could count.

He'd learned perseverance, respect for the old ways of preparing food, long-held family recipes, rare spices, and the basic drive of any good chef: a love for food. Once he'd crossed Europe, he went on to South East Asia, then on to Africa and South America. It had taken him almost three years, but he returned home to New York ready to take on his future as a chef.

Of course, his father was a bit less excited about his career choice. The old man probably hoped Alexander would've gotten over his foodie phase by the time he returned. Fifteen years later, two Michelin Stars and the honor of being an executive chef to a choice few of the world's most renowned restaurants helped to convince his father this was Alexander's true path.

Thankfully, his sister ended up with the skills for making money and a mind for business. Jillian was amazing when it came to numbers and people. She firmly believed in their father's vision, and was now being mentored to take over once the old man stepped down.

Alexander had no interest in the business of money and how to make more of it. However, he had a knack for the charity side of their work, which gave his family a niche to highlight their work. The family had long since accepted his decision to be hands-off, preferring to contribute by cooking and working with the charities they sponsored.

His entire family was back East, and he missed them all, but he'd given his word to Saint, the owner of The Gates, and he'd never go back on it. Oddly, Alexander had chosen this specific restaurant due in part to a conversation he'd had with a diner he'd been called out of his kitchen to meet.

It had been one of the last dinner seating's Alexander had prepared in his last restaurant before recommending his sous chef take over the helm while Alexander moved on to his next adventure. The table the waitress had led him to held four older ladies dressed in their finest for a night on the town in The Big Apple.

The friendly group was from a town named Brighton, in Texas. Rose did most of the talking while the others put their comments in here or there. The older woman preferred to be called Grandma Rose for some reason, and he'd gone with it. After the accolades about his food, the conversation took a sudden turn to his future.

Sure, lots of people came into the restaurant knowing he was notorious for making a place famous, then moving on to do it again. But Grandma Rose was selling a new job like she was getting a finder's fee. At first, he graciously refused, saying he wasn't sure which direction he wanted to go. Without missing a beat, the older woman stated bluntly, "West," and handed him a business card and a picture.

The building was beautiful. Old Hollywood glamor left to fade in the Californian sun. Her mentioning the owner was restoring the building to its former glory made Alexander curious. When he got home later that evening, he looked into DTLA. If the restaurant was part of a club, he was out.

It wasn't long after he'd spoken with the owner, Saint Jeffries that he flew out to LA for a visit. One step inside the building had been enough. Alexander saw Saint's vision clearly, and decided right then and there that he wanted to become part of it, much to Saint's surprise. When Alexander mentioned being visited by Grandma Rose, Saint nodded his head and laughed deeply while mumbling something about miracles.

Alexander should've cut ties with Cooper before moving to LA, but they'd been together for a couple of years by then, and Alexander wasn't one to easily give up on something or someone. Typically, that was a good quality to have, except when it came to people who took advantage of his patient nature.

"To hell with that," he said while letting out a deep breath and leaning his head back against the couch cushions.

His phone rang, and he pulled it out of his pocket to check who was calling. If it was Cooper, Alexander would block the number. Something he should've done the minute the door shut and Cooper was on the other side of it.

No. Jillian, his sister. "Hello, princess," Alexander joked. As a child, he'd been suckered into playing castle with his sister one too many times.

"Good day to you, fine, sir. My spies have told me of a great turmoil in your lands." Jillian's British accent sucked, but she tried.

"That turmoil has been dealt with, fine lady, in a most terminal of ways."

"No, not that," she gasped.

"Yes. Exile from my lands from this day forth."

"Shit, you finally did it," Jillian said, coming out of character. "I'm so proud of you."

"Go me," Alexander grumbled. "Your network works fast."

"I pay them well," she laughed. "You can't be sad that Cooper's gone?"

"No, not truly. It was over long ago," he admitted. "Now, I'm back to being single at thirty-five. I don't like my odds."

"Yeah, I gotta admit, bro, you're over the hill," Jillian teased.

"Asshole," he shot back.

"Love you too. Now get that pessimistic shit out of your head and get your spare bedroom ready. I'm coming for a visit."

"I'm fine. A little down, that's all. You don't have to come out to check on your baby brother." Seriously, the relationship with Cooper had been rocky since before they moved out to LA.

"Check on you? No way. I need a holiday, and California sounds like the perfect place for it to happen."

"But you don't like the heat."

"It's November. Just get my room ready, dufus."

"Dufus? Haven't we gotten past name-calling?" He loved riling up his sister.

"You'll always be my little brother," she said with a healthy dose of love in her tone. "See you Monday."

"See you Monday," Alexander agreed before disconnecting the call.

Slowly, and not without a few groans, he pulled himself up off the couch and headed for the spare bedroom. Alexander would need a good night's sleep before dealing with everything tomorrow, including ordering new furniture for his master bedroom, especially a new mattress. He wanted nothing of his life with Cooper, and that had nothing to do with sentimentality. Alexander was ready for a fresh start. In fact, he was feeling calm already. His sister was right. He should've manned up and broken it off with Cooper a year ago.

Another lesson learned he wouldn't soon forget.

# Chapter Three

"Why can't you leave me alone? I can't do it. Face it. I'm never going to be able to do it."

Sawyer had heard those same words over the last couple of years, and he no longer responded to them. Instead, he placed the cup back onto the tray attached to Bobby's wheelchair. Then Sawyer carried on with cutting the grilled chicken breast into smaller manageable pieces for his brother to eat.

He was meticulous about Bobby's diet. Always doublechecking to make sure to give his brother the best food possible for him to stay healthy. Proteins, fresh fruit, vegetables, and whole grains were staples on Bobby's menu. However, when it came to himself, Sawyer ate whatever was the easiest to prepare and cheapest to buy.

He wasn't the one stuck in that damn wheelchair. His brother deserved the best to stay strong.

"How'd you like the grilled carrots?" he asked, trying to move on to a new, less volatile topic. Marian had gone all out with his "doggie bag." Grilled chicken and vegetables, rolls, two baked potatoes, and a container of mushroom risotto. He'd have to thank her again on Monday.

"They were fine," Bobby said in one of his frequently used, over-exaggerated, and melancholy voices. Think depressed sloth customer service agent. "Everything...is...fine."

His brother had worked hard trying to regain what movement he had, but it was time to try a few more demanding tasks. The first was holding onto a modified plastic cup during mealtime instead of drinking from a long straw sticking out from his tumbler attached to the wheelchair's armrest.

With spinal injuries to C7 and C8, Bobby had been rendered nearly entirely quadriplegic but retained partial control of his chest and arms, and full control of his head. He could control his diaphragm, allowing him to breathe unaided, as well as having limited mobility in his arms and hands.

It had been a hard recovery coupled with losing their mom and dad, but now he was getting healthy, and they were full speed ahead. Sawyer was hellbent on having Bobby gain a bit more freedom. Navigating in Bobby's world took a hell of a lot more concentration and patience than ever before.

"You'll love Alexander's grilled chicken. I don't know what they marinate it in, but it's delicious." Sawyer wasn't going to allow Bobby's attitude to change Sawyer's plans for the day. "You excited about going to Griffith Park?"

That reminded him to look at his watch. Access, a paratransit service in Los Angeles County, would be picking them up in a little over an hour. Leaving them with no room to mess around if they planned on making it in time. Sawyer had made the reservation for this ride weeks ago, so he'd be pissed if they missed it. The vehicle would have a wheelchair lift inside of it, which was mandatory for Bobby's needs. LA's mass transit couldn't accommodate him.

If they wanted to do anything it all had to be planned out beforehand. From figuring out how they would get there to medications, food, and supplies to take along. All the logistics were on Sawyer. Spontaneity hadn't been a thing for many years.

"Alexander, eh," Bobby's voice perked up. "Isn't he the one who chewed you out for the dessert disaster?"

"Yeah, that's the guy. I don't blame him, though. That tray of desserts had to be worth over a hundred dollars." Sawyer wasn't sure why he was making excuses for the man.

"Still, it was an accident," Bobby argued. "The asshole can stuff that dessert right up his ass."

"Bobby."

"What? I'm seventeen. I can get a whole lot more vulgar than that, bro."

"Trust me, I know, and so can I, but we're trying to tone down the more colorful parts of your vocabulary before you start school. But, I appreciate you having my back."

"You'll always have it, and how many times do I need to tell you I don't need to go to some school. What are they going to teach me I don't already know? Lesson one through ten million: Life sucks. Get on with it."

"They'll help with your mobility concerns and be able to teach you new ways of doing things I can't." Like his doctors repeatedly told him, "All spinal cord injuries were different." Who knew what Bobby could gain back in some modified way?

"I have Janice. She comes in five days a week."

"Janice is your home care worker. She isn't a therapist or nurse. School has classes to improve what movement you have and, who knows how many more you could gain? There'll be other people there going through the same things you are. People with shared experiences for you to talk to."

"I talk to you and Janice, and the Garnet's next door," Bobby said with a nod of his head.

"Great four people," Sawyer said with a huff.

"How many people do you talk to regularly who aren't work-related?"

Sawyer thought about it, and if work didn't count, he had the same four, and Miss Chiffon. "Five."

Bobby broke out laughing, and Sawyer couldn't stop himself from joining in. They were a couple of antisocial assholes, but it wasn't by choice. Between all of his responsibilities and a full-time job, he was stretched thin. Socializing wasn't even on his to-do list.

Sawyer leaned down to look his brother in the eye. "You're what's important to me, and you deserve to have the best. That includes friends. I'll promise you something. If you are still absolutely hating it after the first three months, I will remove you from the program. Deal?"

Bobby looked up at him, those dark brown eyes locked on his. "Deal."

"Thank you," Sawyer said before standing up, adjusting his bum leg and placing the bowl of chicken and risotto down in front of Bobby before attaching the plate guard, so the food stayed on the plate when his brother tried to scoop it up.

With a few quick moves, Sawyer slid a universal cuff onto a spoon and attached it to his brother's right hand. The specially designed rubber band allowed Bobby to eat independently, even if he couldn't grab the utensil with his fingers. Sawyer stayed up to date with all new advances in assistive devices. Some were complex, others, like the band, were simple, but if it made his brother's life easier, it was his.

Unfortunately, his bank account couldn't always afford what was needed. Sure, they had the life insurance payments from their parents' death—the same car accident that left both brothers physically damaged—but that went to pay the rent, food, home care, and medical bills.

That's why he worked as much as he could. If Sawyer still didn't have the money, he swallowed his pride and approached organizations like The Triumph Foundation and other spinal cord injury charities for help. He wouldn't allow his brother to miss out because Sawyer didn't make enough money.

Having Janice was a godsend, and her pay was subsidized by the insurance company, allowing Sawyer to work and keep most of his money for the extras in his brother's life. There was a yearly deductible that needed to be paid first, but one-thousand dollars was worlds away from the actual costs, which could run into the hundreds of thousands of dollars yearly.

"Mmmm, this Alexander might be onto something. If you keep bringing me food like this, I may forgive him for being a jerk to you." Bobby chuckled in between bites of his lunch.

"Gee, thanks. Sold out for a chicken."

"Have you tasted this chicken?"

"Shut up and eat while I clean up. Then we have an afternoon of adventure waiting for us." Sawyer jockeyed around the kitchen by holding onto the counter. He'd put on his brace before they left. It wasn't all that comfortable.

"Aye, Aye, Captain," Bobby joked with a slight lift of his fork in salute.

Sawyer huffed. If he were truly the captain, then he'd have been keelhauled by now. He couldn't kick a tire downhill properly.

*** 

Ninety minutes later, they were standing on the grass-covered grounds of Griffith Park. The iconic LA location of over four-thousand acres was five times the size of Central Park. The location housed the LA Zoo, the Griffith Observatory, the Autry Museum of the American West, a golf course, miles of hiking trails, parks, and the landmark Hollywood sign on Mount Hollywood.

However, their destination wasn't the Observatory or the Hollywood sign, but the LA Zoo. Bobby loved wandering around the zoological park and gardens. The animals didn't judge and always managed to calm his brother. Sawyer made sure to take him there a couple of times a month, if not more, when possible.

That was one thing he splurged on, getting Bobby a yearly membership to the zoo so that he and a guest, either Sawyer or Janice, could go whenever they wanted. Provided they made the necessary travel arrangements, of course.

Bobby turned his powered wheelchair onto the entry plaza and rolled underneath the large zoo sign. His brother learned to control his chair like an extension of his body, giving him the freedom to lead the way on their adventures. Sawyer wanted that freedom for Bobby. He'd lost so much.

"Speed up, Sawyer," Bobby yelled over his shoulder. "The bird show is starting in fifteen minutes."

Sawyer hefted his backpack higher on his back, tightened his leg brace, and took off after his animal crazed brother. He couldn't help but laugh as people cleared a path for the speed demon coming through. He should paint flames on his brother's wheelchair and add a breath-controlled horn before Bobby ran someone over. By the time Sawyer reached the bird theatre, his brother was down front talking to one of the handlers in the middle of a group of about five people.

Sawyer knew that if the accident hadn't happened, Bobby would be getting ready to go to college and taking the world by storm. His brother drew people to him, even though Bobby preferred to keep everyone at a distance. The zoo brought out a different side of him, the fun-loving, free-spirited young man Sawyer remembered from "before."

"Look, Sawyer, a California Condor," Bobby called to him. "Come see him. They're critically endangered."

Seats were filling up fast, and Sawyer noticed a few cameras being set up. He placed his backpack on a bench close to the stage and went to his brother, who was laughing and having the time of his life. The animal keepers knew Bobby and always took a few minutes with him if they could.

The condor was stunning. Pure black feathers with white triangular plumage under its wings that spanned over nine feet. Its grey legs and feet led to impressive talons, and Sawyer noticed the middle toe was elongated as the talons pointed straight out and were blunt instead of curved like other birds of prey. He'd been told this genetic difference made it easier for the condor to walk on the ground when scavenging.

The condor turned its bald head toward Sawyer, showing off its sharp ivory beak, and it began staring down both of them with those reddish-brown eyes as if they were the ones on display. Who knew? Maybe they were.

"Hello, Ms. Fields," Sawyer said as he joined them. "I see my brother has made himself at home again."

Ms. Fields had been with the bird show for years and always managed some time for Bobby. When they came here with their parents, Ms. Fields was a part of the crew that cared for the birds. Now, she ran the place. It couldn't have happened to a nicer person.

"Bobby is always welcome here." She laughed. "You two are like part of the family."

"We'd be here every day if we could," Bobby told her.

The small group of people standing behind Ms. Fields stopped talking and turned to face them. Sawyer had to blink several times to make sure he wasn't seeing things because sure as shit, Alexander was standing only feet away in a finely tailored suit.

"I'd like to introduce you two to three of our generous donors in our fight to save the California condor. Alexander Larsen, Janet Barkley, and Cooper Hitchford," Ms. Fields announced, her excitement barely contained. "This is Sawyer Hudson and his brother Bobby. Two of our most loyal of members."

Alexander's smile widened as he recognized Sawyer. "Hello, Sawyer. It's nice to see you out. I thought you lived at work," the larger man teased.

"You know each other?" the one named Cooper asked. Nothing could hide the bleached blond's disgust. This wasn't going well.

"We work together," Alexander provided.

"Wait a minute," Bobby spoke up. "Are you the chef over at The Gates?"

"I am." Alexander's smile widened as if the thought of Sawyer speaking about him was some sort of win.

*Oh, shit.*

"So, you're the asshole who yelled at my brother over an accident," Bobby went off like a firecracker.

"What?" His smile vanished.

"Yeah. The tray of desserts that was knocked to the ground. Ring any bells?" His brother wasn't holding back or letting this go.

"I'm sorry," Sawyer said, knowing this would be the last nail in his employment coffin. Bobby's caseworker was going to flip. "He doesn't mean anything by it."

"The hell I don't," Bobby growled. Sawyer knew his brother would have been right up in Alexander's face if he could stand.

"This is fun." Cooper laughed. "It's finally getting interesting around here. So, you were saying Alexander is an asshole."

"Um, the theatre is full, and it's almost showtime," Ms. Fields said, looking ready to pass out.

"Yes, of course. We'll sit in the audience and discuss this after the show," Alexander instructed as he motioned them toward the reserved front row.

Bobby silently turned his wheelchair around before taking a spot at the bench's end instead of in the reserved section. Sawyer grabbed his backpack and followed his brother.

Once everyone was seated, and he and his brother were away from Alexander's group, Sawyer quietly lost his shit.

"I needed that job, Bobby."

"You shouldn't have to work under someone who belittles you."

"No one should. However, the reality is much harsher than fiction. Without that extra income, we're going to have to cut back until I find another job." Sawyer was already working the changes out in his mind.

For the first time, Sawyer saw regret in his brother's expression. "I'm sorry. I didn't mean for you to get fired. I wanted to stick up for you."

Sawyer reached over and took his brother's left hand. The rigid set of Bobby's fingers made his hand mobility a challenge. "I know. We have to be strong for each other, and you're the best brother I have," he teased, hoping to lighten the mood.

Nothing could be done about it now. What was done was done. Why let it ruin the day with Bobby and the zoo? It wasn't the first time he'd been fired, and Sawyer was sure it wouldn't be the last.

He'd have to pick up a few newspapers on the way home and cruise the online job sites tonight.

"I'm your only brother," Bobby said, followed by an indignant huff any Hollywood star would be proud of pulling off.

"The only—the best. Potato—potahto."

With a genuine smile, they turned back to the bird show. Sawyer chanced a glance over at Alexander and locked eyes with him almost instantly. A crystal-clear blue stare burrowed into Sawyer as he felt his brows furrow. Unless he was mistaken, there wasn't any animosity in his expression, only concern.

Weird. Maybe Sawyer saw what he wanted to see. He'd been known to do that at times, with varying results. This time, no flight of fancy, or intervening supervisor was going to stop the gavel from coming down on him. He needed to accept that.

# Chapter Four

Alexander fought his need to go over to Sawyer and finish their discussion. Had he been abusive toward him? He felt his stomach rolling at the thought. It was possible he'd been cross and hadn't meant it to be so tough. Or, he was one truly giant asshole who'd just gotten told off by Sawyer's brother, Bobby.

He didn't even know the guy had a brother, let alone one with special needs. Come to think about it, Sawyer never talked about personal stuff at work, and Alexander wondered if the injury to Sawyer's leg was related to why his brother needed that wheelchair.

"Stop staring. It's creepy," Cooper whispered. "Seems like I'm not the only asshole in this relationship."

"We're no longer in a relationship. Your family donates to the zoo, and so does mine. You're here because I wouldn't return your calls, and you knew I'd be here." The self-centered hypocrite wouldn't have even bothered with this ceremony for any other reason.

"You doubt my conviction to the condors?" Cooper's soft gasp and his fluttering fingers covering his enhanced pout screamed drama queen. "I'm all for the feathered fuckers getting it on to save the species."

Janet Barkley, the third donor in attendance from the Barkley Foundation, was pulling off the perfect disapproving side-eye at the two of them, and Alexander quickly mouthed the word *sorry* to her. Cooper may not care about the plight of endangered animals, but Alexander did, and so did many others.

Alexander focused all of his attention on the speaker, the condor's handler, and the stunning bird. Cooper would be a departing nuisance. His attendance wasn't what surprised Alexander about today's outing. These feelings of guilt over how he treated Sawyer were what was catching him off guard.

After the speaker was finished answering questions about the magnificent bird's plight, the three donors were called up to say a few words. He smiled at the cameras, as he'd been schooled since birth. Then Alexander renewed his family's pledge to donate to the California condor research the zoo had begun decades ago. After a round of applause, he walked off the stage and headed directly to Sawyer and Bobby. The other donors could field the press on their own.

He sat down on the bench next to Sawyer and said, "Lay it on me. Was I an asshole?"

"Yes," Bobby said without qualm, but Sawyer remained silently staring straight ahead.

"Sawyer?"

"You honestly don't remember?" Sawyer asked when he finally looked up at him. "Something that has shaped my behavior at work ever since isn't even a memory for you."

"I'm sorry. Could you tell me when this happened?" Maybe if Alexander had a date, it would help.

"Last week. Tuesday," Sawyer provided.

"Man, that was only slightly over a week ago. Your head so far up in the air that yelling at someone doesn't mean shit to you?" Bobby asked, accompanied by a disbelieving look. "The rich need therapy."

"Oh, shit," Alexander said before he had a chance to censor himself.

As he searched his recollection of that evening, he remembered earlier in the day he'd been informed about Cooper's threats to the staff who worked in the condo's building. Odds would be good Alexander had been on his last nerve that night. He remembered the loud crash outside the kitchen. When he investigated, Alexander found a waiter and Sawyer tangled up in a heap on the floor covered in chocolate ganache, fresh fruit, and cake made from one of the finest cocoas he could get from South America. He'd waited weeks to receive that ingredient.

The twenty-four-carat gold leaf used to decorate the individual cakes had been stomped into the tile flooring alongside the delicate chocolate artwork that took hours to create. The sight might have sent him over the edge even though he still wasn't sure what he'd said. Considering all that had happened that day, he probably let loose. Alexander was in the wrong, no matter the reason.

"What? You remember," Sawyer asked.

Alexander raked his hand over his face. "I'm an asshole."

"He finally admits it," Bobby cheered. "You going to get my brother fired? You know, he can get a job anywhere. He doesn't need The Gates. But, he doesn't want to leave you high and dry either, so let's call it a wash."

Sawyer looked at his brother with his mouth open. "Who are you?"

Bobby raised his chin. "Your counsel."

Alexander liked the young man's candor. "No. No, it's not a wash."

Sawyer's face fell.

"Your job is safe, Sawyer, but I owe you an apology. I should never have berated you like that. Please forgive me," Alexander said, feeling truly remorseful. He wasn't a cruel

person, and knowing he'd caused Sawyer to change his routine and fear him gutted Alexander.

"You're not going to make up some sort of excuse for your behavior?" Sawyer asked, his voice laced with a fair bit of confusion.

"There's no excuse for treating someone badly. There may be reasons that exacerbated my emotions at the time, but that being said, I still had no right."

"Really?" Bobby asked, looking confused like his brother.

"Yes," Alexander stated confidently. "I'll have to make it up to you. I'll think about how, if that works for you and your counsel."

Sawyer was considering the offer, and Bobby was smiling when a voice Alexander was beginning to despise interjected, "Oh, give them some money and send them on their way. They look like they could use it." Cooper's voice cut in like a knife. "Your family is worth billions. I'm sure they'd never notice a few bucks to help the less fortunate. Maybe you can get spiffy new wheels. What'll it take? A couple of thousand."

Sawyer's face turned red, and he was up out of his seat before Alexander could say a word.

"Who the hell do you think you are insulting my brother like that?" 'Spiffy new wheels.' What the fuck is wrong with you, man?"

Sawyer growled, standing face to face with Cooper. Alexander hadn't heard the man say so much at one time, and they'd worked in the same place for months.

"I'm sorry, Sawyer, Bobby," Alexander said as he stood. "Cooper, go away. You're embarrassing yourself by being the same asshole you've always been."

"You two know each other?" Bobby asked, using his shoulder muscles to move his stiff arm to gesture between him and Cooper."

"As close as lovers can," Cooper flaunted, but then did something Alexander would have never imagined his ex would ever do. He mimicked Bobby's stiff, jerky movements while pointing between himself and Alexander.

He'd been so shocked by Cooper's behavior that Alexander didn't have time to stop Sawyer from lunging forward and delivering one hell of an uppercut to Cooper's jaw. "Don't make fun of my brother, fucker."

Cooper cried out, "Not my face." Before grabbing his jaw and bending over. "Call the police. I want him arrested."

Cameras started clicking, bringing reality into sharp focus by reminding Alexander the press was still mingling around the event. Shit. He quickly bent over and whispered into Cooper's ear. "Don't even think about it."

Cooper stood straight and looked Alexander in the eyes. "Fuck you."

"Then you force me to be a witness for Sawyer. I'll tell anyone who will listen about what you did to cause Sawyer to hit you. I'm sure your family would love that you degraded a disabled person spread across the headlines."

Sawyer and Bobby looked ready to bolt. Moments before the press set upon them, Alexander wrapped his arm around Sawyer's shoulders and began laughing.

"Mr. Hitchford, are you all right, sir?" one reporter asked before shoving a microphone in front of Cooper's angry face.

Alexander took the opportunity to lead the narrative. "Of course, he's okay. It was simply two old friends settling a disagreement. Cooper will tell you the same."

He looked over at Cooper's red face and waited for him to make his choice. Alexander would defend Sawyer and Bobby no question if Cooper chose wrong, but he didn't want Sawyer saddled with an assault charge.

After a few tense seconds, Cooper broke out into a wide smile and began laughing along. "It was nothing. All in good fun. We do this all the time. You see, Sawyer here is an old college buddy of mine, or was, before he dropped out. Just couldn't cut it."

Cooper still had to disparage Sawyer somehow if he couldn't have him charged. The press continued with questions as they followed Cooper back toward the stage. The guy loved the limelight, so he could have it.

"Thank you," Sawyer said. "Bobby, we should get moving if we want to see the lions today." In other words, they were out of there.

"Wait," Alexander began, but this time he was cut off by Ms. Fields. Was the universe working against him?

"Mr. Larsen, would you please join Mr. Hitchford on the stage? The people from the press are waiting to take the group photo." The woman looked unsure of how close to get in case anything else happened. "Bobby, are you and your brother okay?"

"Yes, ma'am."

Cooper caught Alexander's eye when he looked over at the crowd. Cooper's ugly grin was unmistakable. This wasn't over. However, when Alexander turned back around to ask Sawyer and his brother if they could wait to talk this out, and so he could apologize profusely for Cooper's behavior, they were already on their way up the ramp leading toward the exit.

Alexander let out a deep breath and followed Ms. Fields to the stage.

"Oh, dear, my old buddy had to leave so soon." Cooper's snide comment drove home the fact that Alexander had been an idiot for waiting this long to be rid of the cruel man.

"Thanks for reminding me," Alexander said as they were placed behind the condor and alongside the third donor, Ms. Fields, and the handlers.

Cooper's brows pulled together. "Reminding you about what?'

"Why I no longer want your poison in my life," Alexander replied before turning to smile at the photographers.

With any luck, he'd be able to speak with Sawyer at work on Monday and clear this whole thing up. Having the man think of him as an asshole struck deep. Having his ex taunt and make fun of a disabled person was inexcusable.

Alexander wouldn't rest until he'd repaired the damage.

\*\*\*

What the hell was he going to do about work on Monday? There was little doubt in his mind that Alexander would want to continue their conversation at The Gates. They were almost at the giraffe enclosure, and Sawyer was still fuming. They'd worked hard to get a day out at the zoo, so there was no way they were leaving because that Cooper guy was an asshole. How dare he make fun of his brother?

"I hate people with money," Bobby said after being silent for over ten minutes. "They think they're so much better than we are."

"Like throwing money at things will fix it," Sawyer agreed.

"And assuming we're poor," Bobby continued.

"Well, that's not too far off the mark, bro." Sawyer laughed, causing Bobby to join in.

"We may be a little short on cash, but we have everything we need," Bobby declared.

"Damn straight," Sawyer growled. "It's our lives, and we're happy."

The brothers stopped outside the giraffe enclosure to watch the majestic animals as they ate their packed sandwiches, and Sawyer refilled Bobby's tumbler with water from the bottles Sawyer had brought in his backpack. Bobby could hold onto his sandwich and bring it to his mouth, albeit shakily and with a great deal of concentration, and refused help.

Sawyer growled with frustration. He'd already wasted enough time thinking about the bullshit that went down. He refused to let that continue.

"Do you want a churro?" Sawyer asked. "We can grab one at the Churro Factory after we stop to see the gorillas."

His brother's face lit up. "With the chocolate sauce?"

"Why not, let's go all out." Sawyer laughed and immediately felt a bit better even though the knuckles on his right hand throbbed, and he looked down.

"You'd better clean out those cuts before you get a fight bite infection," Bobby advised.

"Agreed," Sawyer said. "Who knows what he's had in that mouth."

"By the sounds of it, Alexander."

"Seriously? Now we need to find a bathroom immediately. Where's the hand sanitizer?" Sawyer asked as he began rifling through his backpack. "Here it is." Why did the thought of Alexander with Cooper seem so offensive?

Sawyer opened the lid and squirted the gel all over his knuckles. It stung, and he winced. Bobby began to laugh, making Sawyer stop shaking his hand. He was acting like this was the first fist fight he'd ever been in. No one lived where they did not knowing how to defend themselves.

"He made fun of you," he growled. "Fucker's lucky I didn't keep going."

"He is an asshole, but I'm beginning to wonder if this chef of yours is," Bobby said as his eyes squinted in thought.

"Chef of mine?" Sawyer coughed, almost gagging on the water he'd been drinking. "Since when?"

"Since your eyes lit up when the big guy put his arm around you. At least we know he's gay. That's a bonus." Bobby's smile was wide as if that were a selling point and made up for everything else.

"My eyes didn't light up. That was anger. Alexander was putting on a show for the press." Nothing more.

"I wonder why he stood up for us," Bobby continued. "He didn't have to do that."

"Maybe he didn't want the event to be ruined, or get bad press." Sawyer hadn't wanted the event to be ruined either. Endangered species need all the help they could get. As for Alexander's bad press, that was his problem.

"Maybe you're right. Either way, it was one hell of an exciting day." Bobby's smile was infectious. He'd always been in some kind of trouble when their parents were alive.

Sawyer leaned against his brother's wheelchair as keepers brought food out and set it in different areas of the habitat safely away from the animals as not to disturb them.

"You got me there," Sawyer agreed. The two of them had been stuck to such a rigid routine that excitement was hard to come by.

They watched the graceful animals as they ate their lunch. Their long, spotted necks and legs seemed to move in a coordinated dance, carefully keeping the baby giraffe in the area of safety between them.

"Do you think you'll still get into trouble?" Bobby asked with genuine concern.

"No, I'm sure everything will be fine." The last thing he wanted was for his brother to worry or feel guilty. Things would not be fine.

"I shouldn't have said anything," Bobby groaned. "I was so mad at the way he treated you. You're the best, and didn't deserve to be yelled at."

Sawyer looked down into Bobby's worried eyes. "If you didn't, then you wouldn't be the brother I know and love. None of what happened is your fault. That Cooper guy was jonesin' for a scene the moment he saw us talking to Alexander." Sawyer had seen the guy circling like a shark looking for his moment to attack.

"He seems like the kind of guy who needs all of the attention on him," Bobby said while slowly shaking his head. "I guess when Cooper's ex ignored him, we became his target,"

"Oh yeah. For sure, bro. Thankfully, we will never have to cross paths with him again."

"I hope," Bobby said.

So did Sawyer. However, he'd keep that to himself. "No worries. We don't run in the same circles as Cooper." And never would. "The chances are slim to none that we'll ever hear his name again."

# Chapter Five

Shit, he needed to play the lottery because slim to none odds were suddenly paying out.

Sawyer held the newspaper Janice had brought with her Monday afternoon before he left for work. This couldn't be happening to them. There was no doubt in his mind he'd be receiving a call from his caseworker and the insurance company at some point today. They'd been pushing to put Bobby into an institution where they didn't have to worry about him anymore. They could wash their hands of him.

Those were the bureaucrats he feared. They'd claim that Sawyer couldn't care for his brother properly and use it to strengthen their case. He had a caseworker from the DCHS checking in with them every month. Rachel seemed like a nice enough lady, but she worked for the enemy trying to take Bobby away from Sawyer's care.

The headline, "Fistfight at the LA Zoo," stood out in big, bold letters on the top of the society page, along with a picture of him and Bobby standing by while Cooper held his jaw.

"Great, absolutely fucking great," Sawyer spat out as he stuffed the newspaper into his backpack. "Don't tell Bobby. He'll worry."

"I've got your back, man. Whatever that guy did, he must've deserved it because I know you haven't been to college with that asshole," Janice said with conviction.

"The bastard was making fun of Bobby," Sawyer hissed between clenched teeth.

"Oh shit, he didn't. I would have punched the dude until he couldn't stand," Janice said while balling her fists.

"I thought about it myself. The college story was simply another attempt at embarrassing me with that dropout comment. But, it saved me from being arrested and charged with assault."

"Oh god, the insurance company would have been all over that." Janice's face paled.

"They still might. We'll have to wait and see. With any luck, they don't read this section of the newspaper." Sawyer knew he wasn't that lucky.

"Okay, I got you covered here. Go to work and try not to worry too much."

"Thank you, Janice. You've been a lifesaver since the beginning. I don't know what we would do without you." Sawyer meant every word. The woman had become part of the family.

"You're sweet, but I know the two of you would do fine without me. You're a strong team. Nobody could break that," Janice said as she pushed a stray purple hank of hair away from her face. Bobby's health-care aide was a free spirit. She changed the color of her brightly colored hair regularly and seemed to get new piercings or tattoos all the time.

"I hope so." He wished the insurance company understood that.

The sound of Bobby's wheelchair motor was heading their way, so Sawyer quickly zipped his bag shut and plastered on a neutral facial expression.

"So, I'm off to work," Sawyer said as he reached for his apartment keys.

"Okay. I'll see you in the morning," Bobby said as he rolled by. He had his red mesh bag full of assistive gaming controllers that could be attached to his wheelchair so he could play modified video games. They hadn't come cheap, but the games kept Bobby moving and entertained. To Sawyer, they were worth every penny.

"Are you going to let Janice win a few tonight?" Sawyer asked while grabbing his jacket off the hook.

"C'mon. Where'd the fun be in that?" his brother teased as he positioned himself in front of the empty entertainment unit that held only their small television. Sawyer had picked up the gaming system second hand at a pawn shop. Only Bobby's controllers were new.

"That'll be the day." Janice laughed as she went to attach the controllers. "One of these times, I'm going to break out some moves you ain't never seen before."

Sawyer couldn't help but laugh at the two of them. They were both competitive, and it was fun watching them play against one another. So much trash talk, the likes that had never been heard outside these walls, thankfully, or he'd be looking for a new apartment.

"Okay, you two, be good." Sawyer waved from the hallway before stepping out his front door and locking it behind him. He sucked in a deep breath and steeled himself for the day ahead.

Once he hit the alley, Sawyer pulled the newspaper out from his backpack and began reading.

*Cooper Hitchford was involved in a physical altercation with a strange man on Sunday outside the California condor exhibit at the LA Zoo. Alexander Larsen, the heir to the Larsen fortune, was seen standing nearby Cooper, his on-again, off-again boyfriend. Although the punch was explained away by Mr. Hitchford as simply "two old friends settling a disagreement," it doesn't ring true for this reporter. Could this have been a lovers' quarrel? Perhaps a love triangle? Who is the man that threw the punch? Stay tuned because this reporter won't rest until we have all the salacious details.*

Lovers' quarrel, what the hell? This can't be happening. Sawyer looked for the reporter's name at the top of the article. Trey Stoneham. A man Sawyer needed to avoid at all costs.

He made it to work without being approached by anyone. He'd kept his eyes on his surroundings, half expecting someone with a camera and microphone to jump out from behind a Dumpster. It wouldn't be long before they figured out who he was and where he lived and worked. Thankfully, their apartment building had a locked security door, requiring people to be buzzed in. Sawyer hoped they'd be safe there. The old lady in apartment 319 buzzed anybody in.

He walked up the steel back steps of The Gates and pushed the buzzer to be let in. The door lock snapped open, and he made his way to the staff area to drop off his backpack and jacket. During the day it didn't get cold, but after four in the afternoon the sun dropped, and the air turned drastically cooler. In a little under a month, they'd be in the Christmas holiday season, and work would get crazy busy. He'd be walking home even later, which meant it would be that much colder.

Sawyer made it as far as hanging his bag and jacket up before Marian came to stand in front of him.

"I'm sorry." That was all he managed to get out before the kind older woman pulled him into her arms and hugged him. He missed getting hugs from his mom, and he couldn't help but sink into the motherly warmth and safety. Sawyer had been forced to grow up fast in order to keep up with his new responsibilities.

"Let's go have a talk in the office," Marian said.

"Yes, ma'am," he agreed and followed her out of the kitchen.

It was over. They'd seen the newspaper article. It was probably splashed all over the internet by now. Who could blame his boss? Sawyer was the one who threw the punch.

Marian opened the office door and ushered him through. Inside the office, a small group of people was waiting. Saint and Max, the owners, Miguel and Finn, the manager, and most surprising of them all, Alexander stood up from his chair when Sawyer and Marian entered the room.

Before anyone got a chance to say anything, Sawyer decided to start. He could at least leave with dignity. "I understand why you've called me in, and I'm sorry for my behavior as it affects my job here, but not the fact that the guy had it coming. You've all been wonderful to me, and I accept your reasons for letting me go." There, done. He knew if there was an option—and he was sure there wasn't since he was a dishwasher, not a famous *rich* chef—between firing him or Alexander, who would get the ax.

"Thank you for your understanding, but I'm afraid we don't work like that around here," Saint stated. "Each employee is important to us. You've been with us for some time now, and there's no way we're losing you because of that asshole."

"What? I'm a dishwasher. We're a dime a dozen."

"No. You're Sawyer Hudson, a valued member of The Gates crew. When we hire people here, we choose them for multiple reasons," Max explained.

"Marian and I are straight off the streets of Skid Row," Finn told him something Sawyer didn't know. "I'd probably be dead if it hadn't been for Saint. Now I'm attending college and managing the bar and restaurant here."

"Alexander was kind enough to explain to us what really happened at the zoo yesterday," Max said, and if the expression on his face was anything to go by, he was pissed.

Sawyer turned to face Alexander. "You did? Why?"

"Because it was the right thing to do." He acted as if everything was so simple. The man was clueless. The right thing for him, maybe. He wasn't going to lose his brother and didn't have the resources to fight the insurance company that'd take him away.

"Okay...." Sawyer was confused. He should've been escorted out of the building already.

"It's going to be fine," Marian said as she patted him on the shoulder and sat down in a nearby chair.

When she crossed her legs, Sawyer could see the hilt of the knife strapped around her ankle. He'd always meant to ask about it, but perhaps the earlier Skid Row comment answered that question. The streets were a hard place to survive.

"How is everything going to be fine?" Sawyer asked as he sat down beside her. "My damn face is in the newspapers because of some sort of love triangle bullshit. Excuse me, ma'am, for my language."

Marion patted him on his shoulder a second time. "I've said worse, sweet boy."

"Has anyone attempted to make contact with you or your brother?" Alexander asked, leaning forward, closer to Sawyer.

"Not yet, but it's only a matter of time." He could feel the doomsday clock ticking in his head.

"Guys, I'm not sure you all want to see this," Finn said, looking down at his cellphone.

"What's wrong now," Sawyer bowed his head and rubbed his fingers along the base of his sore neck. This nightmare was expanding by the minute, along with his headache.

"Mr. Cooper Hitchford held a press conference. He said he wouldn't be charging you with assault because of you... um, you're a poor deranged man to whom he'd offered assistance." Finn's face paled.

"No, no, no, no," Sawyer kept repeating, hoping to wake himself. "All he tried to do was make my brother feel ashamed and worthless."

"That's good he said he wasn't pressing charges, right," Miguel asked, looking for the bright side in this situation.

"You'd think, but you see, this poor deranged man has a little brother who is still under the age of majority, and permanently in a wheelchair, and is pretty much a quadriplegic. On top of that, I'm fighting with an insurance company who's trying to remove Bobby from my care in order to throw him into one of those dead-end institutions. That way, they can wash their hands of him."

"Oh shit," Alexander groaned.

"So your little tiff with your boyfriend has now threatened my family. My brother," Sawyer railed at the man who'd caused all of this.

When had he stood because he was now looking down at a still seated Alexander?

"I'll help figure this out. I won't let your brother be taken away from you," Alexander swore, his pale blue eyes flashed with anger. "My family has an army of lawyers."

Sawyer deflated and sat back down. "Please stay out of it. You've caused enough damage already."

Sawyer's head was beginning to ache harder. Another leftover from the car accident to go along with his leg and his brother's paralysis: migraines. Nasty, painful, vicious episodes following extreme stress. His doctor had prescribed medication to lessen the severity, but at over fifty bucks a pill, he had better things to spend that money on. Though now would be a good time to have had one.

"Are you okay?" Marian asked.

Pinholes of light shot through his vision as the pain worked its way up from the back of his neck before settling in his eyes. Sawyer knew he was squinting but had no other choice to cut out some of the light in the office.

"It's a headache. I should go back to work." The need to get out of there was high.

"It looks like a migraine," Saint said. "How often does this happen?"

"More and more lately," Sawyer replied, sending a glare at the offender who had the decency to look contrite.

"Has your doctor given you anything to help?" Marian asked as she ran to turn off the lights.

"Yes." Technically, he wasn't lying.

"Are they in your backpack? I'll get them," Finn offered.

"No, it's okay. I don't have any."

"You ran out, or you've never had any at all," Finn asked as if understanding Sawyer's reasoning instantly.

"The latter."

The crew exchanged looks, but by now, Sawyer was at his wit's end and was desperate to get out of the room. "I'm sorry. I have to leave."

He stood, and the world tilted. The last thing he remembered was being caught before everything went dark.

# Chapter Six

With great effort, Sawyer pried his eyes open a crack. Mercifully, the room was dark. He reached up and found a cold, wet cloth on his forehead, and then realized he was lying in a bed, but whose?

Slowly he sat up, fighting off a wave of nausea as he attempted to stand. He had to find out where he was. He slid the bedroom curtains back a sliver and saw the lit-up street in front of The Gates below. He was still at work?

He moved closer to the side table and found a pair of sunglasses waiting for him. He glanced at the time on the clock and felt his heart stop. It was almost two in the morning. He had to get home to his brother. He'd never been this late.

Sawyer limped to the door without any thought, pulled it open, and was immediately assaulted with the overhead lighting. He still had the sunglasses in his hand and put them on, shielding his eyes from the glare. Someone from down the hall called for the lights to be turned off.

"Sawyer, you need to stay in the dark until your migraine gets better. The doctor said that was best." As he got closer, Sawyer recognized Finn, who tried to lead him back into the bedroom.

"Doctor? Wait, I have to go home. My brother has to be scared sick that I haven't come home yet." Sawyer struggled to go in the other direction. As a tug of war ensued, his leg brace squealed like a car being crushed before snapping and sending them both to the floor.

"What the fuck else can go wrong?" Sawyer yelled from his position on the ground. Two strong arms lifted and carried him to a nearby couch. He looked up and saw Miguel. Finn followed, apologizing in almost tears for breaking his brace.

"It's not your fault. It was being held together by sheer will alone."

"Sawyer. Sawyer, where are you?" Bobby's voice reached him before his brother's wheelchair rounded the corner of a hallway, and he barreled straight into the living room of wherever they were as people jumped out of his way.

"Bobby, how did you get here?" What's going on? Janice followed Bobby over to Sawyer's side.

"It's okay, bro," Bobby assured. "Your boss came and picked us up after you got sick. Everything is fine. I've got everything under control, so don't worry." His brother looked so proud of himself that Sawyer, who was about to freak out, leaned back to listen.

"When did we change roles," Sawyer asked, so happy that his brother was here and safe that he didn't even question where Saint found a vehicle with a chairlift on a moment's notice.

"When you became incapacitated." He stared at Sawyer. "Brothers watch out for each other," Bobby stated firmly.

"Why did you believe them? You don't know them? They could have been lying." Though he was happy his brother was here safe, it could have gone the other way so easily.

"Alexander was with them," Bobby answered as if that was good enough proof. "They showed Janice their identification and everything."

Sawyer shook his head. "You're way too trusting."

"Sometimes you have to take a chance," his brother said with a nod. "Plus, they brought a cop along."

"A cop? You didn't think to start with that. Why were the police involved?' Great. Exactly what he'd been trying to avoid.

"Don't worry," Marian said, "It's Joey's boyfriend, Sam. He's LAPD, and we thought it would help assure them we weren't weirdos," she explained as if all this wasn't crazy as hell.

"If one more person tells me not to worry," Sawyer grumbled before looking around the room to find concerned expressions on the faces of the same people who were in the office earlier. "Thank you for taking care of me. I don't want to come off as ungrateful or anything. I'm shocked, is all. Where are we exactly?"

"You're still at The Gates upstairs in one of the recently completed condos on the third floor," Saint explained from a chair a few feet away.

Sawyer looked at the sparse furnishings and asked. "Who lives here?" The room had the basics: couch, chairs, wall-unit, television, and artwork, but nothing personal that said someone lived here.

"You do." Marian came closer with a bottle of water she placed in front of him.

He was distracted by the pounding in his head, so it took a moment before her words sunk in. "Me? I don't think so. I'd remember moving."

"I arranged everything, with Saint and Alexander's help." His brother looked so proud of himself; Sawyer had no choice but to smile in response. *Arranged everything?* "You always take care of me, so now it's my turn to take care of you." Sawyer reached out and held his brother's hand.

"We discussed the ongoing situation about Cooper," Max interjected, "the press, and your insurance company and determined it would be safer for you and Bobby to stay in one of the rental units for the time being."

*Do these people think this is normal behavior?*

"Why didn't you tell me about the stuff in the newspaper this morning before you left?" Bobby asked with his brows drawn together.

"Technically, yesterday morning, and I didn't want to worry you," Sawyer stated.

"You don't need to shield me, you know," Bobby argued. "I'm almost an adult."

Yes, he did. That was his job, but Sawyer let it go and went in another direction. "Rentals, but I thought the condo units were for sale only."

"At first, yes. However, we've decided to set a few aside as possible rental incomes for the building," Saint answered as he moved over to sit in a chair opposite Sawyer. "Until this thing with Cooper and the insurance company is figured out, this is the best place for the two of you. There's round the clock security, a separate entrance for you and Bobby with an elevator, and all the backup you could want if you need it."

"You don't have to sell this place to me, it's amazing, but we can't afford this." It sucked to admit that, but there was no way they could come up with the money to rent this place.

"We'll figure something out," Saint assured him as if the rent was a technicality. Was the sky a different color in their worlds?

Sawyer had his mouth already open, ready to decline the offer when Bobby spoke up. "It's perfect and has two bedrooms. You won't have to sleep in your chair in the living room anymore."

He could feel his face warming in embarrassment and hoped no one could see his eyes through the dark sunglasses. He'd kept everything about his life to himself so he wouldn't look pathetic. While he appreciated what these people were trying to do, he hated that expression on their faces of abject concern. He could take care of himself and his brother. He'd been doing it for a couple of years, and he'd do it the rest of his life. Bobby was his family. His only family,

"Janice can come here when you work downstairs. Nothing about that arrangement is going to change. Bonus? You won't have to walk all the way home at night with your hurt leg. There's even a sixty-inch television in my room, bro. Can you imagine the games we can play on that?" Bobby's face glowed with happiness. How could Sawyer take this away from him?"

Sawyer turned to face Saint. "I'll work for free, do maintenance, whatever you need. I'm handy, and I've worked in a lot of different places. I have skills." Sawyer didn't want to be rude, but ordinary people didn't take in people like him and Bobby. They had a shitload of problems and could offer zero benefits.

"No. Working for free isn't work. It's volunteering, and that's not on the table," Saint waved off his offer. "I'm sure we have extra jobs around here that have been lingering, so I'd appreciate the extra help."

"Anything. My parents' life insurance payments covers the rent, Bobby's medical needs, and food. Considering we need to keep our apartment for when this is over, I have nothing else to offer but my services. We don't have the money to keep two places."

Marian handed him a cup of something hot. It smelled like chamomile tea. The warmth seeping into his cold hands felt so good he could almost block out the unrelenting pain in his head. He looked down at his busted brace hanging limply from his leg.

*What now? Maybe I can fix it.*

Before he could even get out the words floating around in his head, Alexander said, "We'll have an Orthotist come by to check and measure your leg for a new brace."

"A new brace and a private visit? That'll cost a whack. Why are you all doing this?" Sawyer looked around at the group. "Bobby and I have been rebuilding our lives for what feels like forever, and no one has ever offered to do anything for us. What's the catch?" *Nobody does anything for free.* It was a harsh lesson he'd learned early on.

Finn smiled wide. "That's what I thought at first when Saint bought the building that I happened to be camping out in. This strange guy comes in and turns my life upside down, and I'm sure he wants something from me. Hell, I even gave him a fake name in the beginning. Larry, or something like that. Took me more than a minute to believe he wasn't angling." He shrugged. "Now, look at me. A student and a manager, and Saint still hasn't asked me for anything but to come to work on time and do a good job."

"It was Larry," Saint laughed. "Feels like so long ago." He got this dreamy look on his face as he took hold of Max's hand. Sawyer had noticed the scars on both of Saint's hands, and Joey, one of the bartenders, had explained about Saint being kidnapped in the jungle while he was a doctor and was trying to help the poor people that lived there. He'd been shot through both hands and in the stomach.

Miguel set a key card on the coffee table and said, "Think about it overnight."

"Overnight? Bobby has specific needs, and all his equipment and our belongings are back at our apartment. We can't have a random sleepover." There was a transfer lift, his hospital bed, CPAP machine, medications, and on and on.

His brother smiled again. "We thought of that. Packed a lot of my stuff, and it's already set up in my room. My hospital bed will be moved tomorrow, and Janice will check to make sure we didn't miss anything. Mr. and Mrs. Garnet are going to keep an eye on our place, and I even packed a bag for you with Alexander's help."

Everything came to a screeching halt in Sawyer's spinning brain. Chef Alexander Larsen had his hands on Sawyer's no-name, cheap clothes. And his underwear? Yep, this day just kept giving and giving.

"Sawyer, I have one question for you," Marian said, getting Sawyer's attention. "Why didn't you sign up for our group medical coverage after your first month here? It would have paid for your migraine medication and help set you up with a new brace."

"I couldn't afford a deduction from my paycheck. We need every penny I make in other areas of our lives." He didn't want to come out and say it was to pay for things Bobby needed that SSI and Social Security didn't cover. The combined monthly payment from both barely paid for the basics. If Sawyer shared that, Bobby would feel like shit, and there was no way Sawyer would allow that to happen.

"I see," Saint said, but Sawyer could tell the boss was already lost in thought. "I wasn't aware it was cost-prohibitive. We'll have to address that with our broker."

"It's a generous plan for the money, sir." What he didn't say, but Saint was not stupid, so he had to hear the implication that Sawyer didn't have the money. He didn't want Saint to feel bad or to think he was ungrateful. The bosses had been nothing but good to Sawyer. "You treat your employees much better than most."

"Thank you." Saint smiled. "I try to think of everything, but I have to admit some things get by me."

"In the meantime, Janice has agreed to stay here for a few whole days to help with the transition. Which is fortunate, especially now with your brace broken," Max said. "We've set up a temporary bed in Bobby's room for her for now, and we will arrange for a walker to be dropped off to help you get around temporarily."

"Wait a minute, I haven't agreed to anything," Sawyer said, overwhelmed by everything that happened while he was passed out. They wrapped it all up in a fancy bow, but it didn't change the situation. Whether they lived here or in their apartment, people will come looking for him.

"Please, Sawyer," Bobby begged while giving him his puppy dog eyes treatment. It wasn't fair how good he was at that. "The kitchen has an island bigger than our whole kitchen in the other place. There's lots of room for my wheelchair to move around. It'd be like a holiday. We never have time for fun. Did you forget the sixty-inch television? I even brought my special controllers."

*Ah shit. Bobby has me pinned against the wall.*

There wasn't a chance in hell Sawyer could say no to him now. Bobby had fallen in love with the idea of staying here. "Fine, but only until this whole mess blows over. This arrangement isn't permanent. You understand that." He'd never be able to scrounge up enough money to afford a place like this.

If his brother could've jumped up and down, he'd be a pogo stick. His smile said it all. "Thank you, bro. It's going to be great. We're going to have so much fun. Who knows, we could be here for Christmas. Can we get a big tree this year? A real one, not fake like the old one in the box at home."

Fun wasn't the word he'd use right now, and Christmas wasn't looking good either, but Sawyer kept that to himself.

He could feel the weight of everything that'd happened in the last twenty-four hours bearing down on him as his migraine threatened a full-blown return. He closed his sore eyes. While the sunglasses helped, they were a stopgap measure that didn't address the larger problem: his pounding head. He began rubbing his temples, searching for relief.

"Is your migraine getting worse again?" Alexander asked as he pulled a bottle from his pants pocket. "I picked this up for you after the doctor came by. It's supposed to help with your migraines. He said for you to put one pill under your tongue and let it melt. It's the same medication as your doctor had originally prescribed." The chef looked exhausted as he uncapped the bottle and tapped a single pill onto his palm before holding it out to Sawyer. "This will help."

"How did you know what my doctor wrote down?" Alexander glanced up at Bobby, who was looking everywhere but at Sawyer. "I should've known."

Sawyer took the small pill and did as Alexander told him to. Once it melted away, he said," Thank you. Now you should go home. You look as tired as I feel." He quickly covered up his concern for the man who'd brought this shit down upon them, to begin with. "You should all be at home."

Alexander cracked the first smile Sawyer had seen since this whole screwup began. "I'm fine, but thank you for your concern."

"Okay, now that that's all settled," Marian announced. "It's time for everybody to go home and leave these men in peace." Considering Max, Saint, and Marian lived downstairs in the hub, they didn't have to go far. Once the fourth floor was done, Saint and

Max would be moving into the penthouse, and Marian would have her one-bedroom apartment.

People stood as Marian remained seated.

"Aren't you coming, Marian?" Saint asked with an amused expression on his face.

"I'll hang around here for a bit to make sure everything is set. The rest of you can hit the road. Janice and I have this covered." She looked like a queen lording over all these men and damned if everyone didn't listen to her and began heading for the front door.

"Good, at least someone does," Sawyer moaned as he pressed his head against the back of the couch. He needed to lie down again.

Moments later, he was lifted into another pair of strong arms. He opened his eyes, expecting Miguel but finding Alexander carrying him back inside the dark bedroom. He laid Sawyer down without saying a word and then brought his canvas bag over from the chair and placed it on the bed beside him.

"There's a bathroom through those doors," Alexander explained. "We'll have a walker here by morning. In the meantime, do you need any help with your brace or clothes, bathroom, anything?"

The way Alexander framed the question and his tone didn't lead Sawyer to believe he was being patronized, but he still felt embarrassed. The last thing he needed was for the handsome chef to help him go to the washroom or look at his fucked-up body.

"No. I'm good. Thank you again for your help." *Please go away.*

Alexander let out a huff. "You're welcome, Sawyer. I never meant for any of this to happen. I'm sorry. You have my word. I'll help you and your brother through this."

Sawyer's response was immediate. "Bobby and I will figure this out. We've been getting by for years." He couldn't help but be defensive. If he acknowledged defeat, everything he'd suffered through would be for nothing. "We always manage to land on our feet."

Instead of acting like he'd been rejected, Alexander chuckled like Sawyer was an amusing kid. What an asshole. "Yes, I imagine you do. Good night, Sawyer."

"Good night, Chef."

Sawyer waited until he heard the front door close before calling out for Marian.

"Yes?" she asked as she stuck her head through the open bedroom door.

"Um...is he gone?"

"He is."

"Can I get you to give me a hand for a sec?"

"Of course," Marian said.

Sawyer could feel his cheeks warming and was glad for the dark room. Sure, he'd dismissed Alexander's attempt to help him. Of all the people he wanted to appear weak in front of, the chef wasn't one of them.

"Thank you, Marian. For real."

"Any time, young man."

# Chapter Seven

Alexander dragged his tired body the last few steps to his front door, tapped his key fob to the door, and walked straight into a pile of luggage. For a fraction of a second, he thought the worse. Cooper had let himself back in. However, Alexander had given the doorman explicit instruction that Mr. Hitchford was no longer living there, and was not allowed upstairs for any reason.

"Where the hell have you been," a female voice shouted from the couch. Jillian sat up and glared at him. "I've been worried senseless. Did you turn off your cellphone?"

Shit. With everything else that was happening, he'd completely forgotten his sister was coming into town. "I'm sorry, Jillie. Things got away from me today."

Her eyes softened, and she stood as he neared. Alexander needed a hug, and Jillian was the perfect person for the job. He held out his arms, and his sister walked straight into them and gave him the comfort he needed.

"What's happened?" She always knew when things weren't right. "Does this have anything to do with that fleabag Cooper?"

All Alexander could do was laugh, and even that sounded hollow. "A lot has happened since the last time we spoke. It's hard to know where to begin."

A change of clothing, a tumbler full of a thirteen-year-old single malt scotch whisky, and a rehash of everything that'd happened, with his sister's stricken look, Alexander waited for her to respond. He felt drained after recounting the sordid details, but at least she was up to speed.

"It's not your fault." Of course, she'd defend him even in this impossible situation.

"Yeah, it is?" Alexander stared at his sister.

"No, it's not. Everything that's happened is Cooper's fault, and whoever these people are who think they can take Bobby away from

Sawyer." He could see his sister's gears turning, figuring things out, and the next steps. Working through the problem was in her wheelhouse, and the gears were grinding.

"Maybe. But I'm the one who drew my ex to them. Cooper didn't appreciate being ignored, so first, he showed up at an event he'd never come to, but since I wasn't taking his calls, he did what he always does. Tries anything to get his way. When he saw I was speaking with people he didn't know, and I had the nerve to pay attention to them and not him... Well, you know the rest."

"Yeah, I do. And you're an asshole."

"Wait? One minute I'm innocent; the next, I'm an asshole. What's with the flip-flop?"

"No, I meant the reason you were speaking to Sawyer and Bobby. Because you'd been a jerk to him at work," she clarified.

"Right. I was trying to apologize. Then all hell broke loose." He took downed the rest of his scotch.

"It was quick thinking on your part to lay it out for Cooper in case he dared to call the police. I knew I didn't like that little shit for a myriad of reasons, but I never thought he'd stoop as low as making fun of a disabled person. Is he on drugs?"

"You meant actually, or as a turn of phrase?"

She shook her head. "Both."

"He's always been...out there. You know that. In actuality, I don't know. The last few months, we've been living like roommates, barely seeing each other, and when we did, we fought. I haven't got the first clue what he did when I was at the restaurant. He'd been more agitated and confrontational in the last six months, blaming me for bringing him to LA as if I dragged him here."

Jillian made an unladylike growl. "That little weasel went with you because no one else would've put up with him as long as you had. I've always said you have the patience of a saint but no sense of self-preservation. So, let's get down to details. What does this Sawyer want from you?"

The question wasn't as cruel as it sounded. Growing up in a well-known wealthy family tended to bring out unbridled greed from a lot of people. A fender bender that most people settled without insurance companies turned into multi-million-dollar lawsuits because the Larsen pockets were extra deep. Jillian had been down that road with her first serious boyfriend. After several months of dating, she learned the guy had a wife and kid in another state and thought he could latch onto some serious money before breaking it off with her.

"Nothing."

"Nothing?" she asked in a disbelieving tone.

"Yeah, well, there's one thing," Alexander admitted.

"Knew it."

"He wants me to leave him alone and stay out of his business." That wasn't going to happen. "He blames me for all this and rightly so."

Jillian's eyebrows drew together as she continued to stare at him. "Are you going to do that?"

"Hell no." He wasn't going to leave those brothers to the mercy of the sharkish media, Cooper's temper tantrum, and a debauched insurance company.

His sister broke out in a smile that left no doubt that she agreed with his choice. "Okay, first we have to shut up Cooper, do media damage control, and get our lawyers on the insurance company." She nodded like she was agreeing with herself. "The attention slut is bound to do more interviews as long as someone from the press keeps listening. We have to make sure no one is listening."

"We? When did you become part of this?"

"The moment you did," she stated plainly. "You'd better call mom and dad and fill them in before they get wind of what happened from the papers."

"They're probably still sleeping. I'll do it when I wake up. I'll call and explain everything," Alexander agreed before emptying the last of his scotch from his glass. "I need to get some sleep, or I'll be useless tomorrow."

"Don't worry, I've got your back," she said as she picked up her laptop from the coffee table.

"Don't start any wars while I'm sleeping, Jillie," Alexander said before leaning over and kissing her on the cheek.

"Now, where would the fun be in that?" She laughed as her laptop came to life and her nimble fingers began dancing over the keys.

Alexander could understand the strong connection between Sawyer and Bobby. He had the same with Jillian, and the thought of her being taken away from him had him convinced he'd do someone bodily harm.

There was no way in hell he'd ever allow that to happen to Sawyer and Bobby. Separating the two would be catastrophic to brothers who'd already suffered so much.

*** 

Sawyer slowly pushed the borrowed walker down the hallway on his way to his brother's room. His new brace would be ready by the beginning of next week, and for him, it couldn't arrive fast enough. It had been a long time since he'd had to rely on a walker to get around, and it brought back painful memories.

Surgeries, depression, disappointment, and fear were woven into this object from the past. Once Sawyer had his final piece of metal surgically implanted, and every last screw, pin, and rod set in place, he took to the full leg brace and never looked back. He needed to hit the ground running to take care of his brother and didn't have time for follow-ups or further surgeries.

There was no way Bobby would be forced to stay in the hospital while they kept trying new therapies and options on Sawyer. The last time he left his doctor, he'd sworn never to go under the knife again, and he hadn't.

What he needed was to get back to work so that he could contribute while staying at The Gates. So far, it seemed like every time he turned around, someone from the crew was bringing over food, groceries, video games for Bobby to play, and all manner of things that *cost money*.

Christmas decorations had been hung all over the condo. Poinsettias, garland, baubles, and bows with multicolored lights blinking happily throughout every room. At first, Sawyer thought to stop them since they'd already done far too much, but he'd allowed them to carry on because his brother's face lit up every time he caught sight of a decoration. There wasn't a tree yet. They still had a month left before the jolly fat man showed.

That brought up another concern, presents. Any other year he'd be taking on as many extra shifts as he would so he could buy presents. Without a paycheck, he wasn't sure what he was going to do.

Alexander had been the only one who steered clear of their temporary digs, as Sawyer had asked. However, a few days of peace had brought with it some clarity. At the time, he'd directed all of his anger at the chef, and blamed him for everything that had happened to Bobby and him.

It was a heavy-handed conclusion and not true. With nothing else to do but replay the series of events that led them to this point, Sawyer recognized the real fault lay with that piece of shit Cooper.

Sawyer had prepared to apologize the next time he saw the chef. But since he'd basically kicked him out, who knew when that would be. Weirder than weird: Sawyer missed seeing the guy.

There was a bit of good news. No reporters had tried to contact him or his brother, and there was no sign of that Trey Stoneham character who wrote the article Sawyer read on his way to work last Monday.

Sawyer thought back to the morning of the day they went to the zoo and remembered how he'd told Bobby he needed more friends to talk to. He couldn't help but laugh softly to himself. At least that didn't seem like a problem anymore. On the contrary, members of the crew dropped by throughout the day without invitation. At times, Sawyer felt put upon, embarrassed, wary, and grateful. He'd never met people like this, and didn't know what to make of them. One thing he couldn't deny: they were good to his brother. Most had been suckered into playing one of Bobby's video games with him, and the brat was undefeated.

As Sawyer neared Bobby's room, he could hear his brother and Janice talking. The topic stopped him in his tracks.

"He'd be better off without me," Bobby's voice shook as he spoke. "Look at the trouble I've got us into this time. Sawyer could do anything he wants if I'm not in the picture. Now he's stuck for the rest of his life taking care of me."

Before Janice had a chance to respond, Sawyer pushed Bobby's bedroom door open and stormed in, or as close to storming as he could do with one good leg and a walker.

"My life would've been over if I didn't have you," Sawyer shouted.

Both Bobby and Janice looked up in shock from where they'd been working on Bobby's daily PT on the carpeted floor. Sawyer made his way over to the chair beside Bobby as Janice lifted his brother and sat him back into his wheelchair, and strapped him in.

"I'll give you two some privacy," she said as she walked out and closed the door behind her.

"Never in a million years would I ever be better off without you. You're my brother. I'd be lost without you." His stomach churned at the thought of a life without Bobby.

"I'm sorry, bro. I didn't mean for you to hear that," he said, his voice barely above a whisper. "But it's true. Look at the shit that's happening to us. We have to hide out from reporters because I couldn't keep my damn mouth shut. None of this would have happened if I weren't around. Maybe it would have been better if I hadn't survived the car crash like mom and dad."

Sawyer felt like he'd been sucker-punched. He couldn't breathe. His mind whirled along with his stomach as he sat, stunned by Bobby's declaration. How long had he been thinking this way? Why hadn't Sawyer noticed?

He got up out of his chair, limped over to his brother to wrap his arms around him. Sawyer could feel the hot tears running down his face, but he didn't care. His brother was in pain, and that knowledge was tearing him apart.

"Never think that. It's awful mom and dad are gone. I can't imagine my life without you. You're my family. You're my little brother. You mean everything to me. If I didn't have you, there would be no life for me to live. You're the only reason I keep going day after day."

Sawyer wished he could reach out and make Bobby feel how true that statement was. There'd been a hand full of times Sawyer could remember when the only thing that stopped him from finding a tall building to jump off of was Bobby.

It'd been a rough couple of years after losing their parents, what with their physical recoveries, navigating insurance companies, Social Security, California SSI, and the only help Sawyer had was a social worker assigned to him at the hospital. She was a godsend. Without her, he had no idea how he would've even known what to do and how to do it. Going from being a teenager heading off to college to setting up a house and figuring out bills, getting work without any employable skills, and making sure his brother had everything he needed to where they were now was a miracle. In truth, it had been hell in the beginning, but over time it all simply became their new reality.

"You could finally have the life a normal twenty-two-year-old deserves, instead of playing nursemaid for me." Bobby's expression begged Sawyer to understand why he felt this way.

"And what kind of life is that?" He'd never been a normal anything. Sawyer had spent most of his teenage years studying to get a scholarship, which made his mom and dad proud he'd be the first in their family to make it to college, and they wouldn't have to shell out the money to send him.

Instead, he'd caused their deaths.

"Clubs, boyfriends, parties, even college. You could check and see if that scholarship you received at Fullerton would be honored considering the accident and everything that's happened since." Bobby's face lit up as he talked about Sawyer's possible future without him. Sawyer felt like he was about to throw up.

"I've always hated clubs. You know that," Sawyer argued. "Boyfriends come and go, and so do those parties. As for college, that was a dream too far. What's important to me is you, my brother, because I love you, man. If I didn't have you, I'd have no reason to stay on this earth. I'd have no one to watch out for me and to love me back. You are my best reason to live." Sawyer's words were torn straight from his heart.

As he leaned his weight against the heavy wheelchair, he continued to hold onto Bobby until his good leg became sore from holding himself up without his walker. Grudgingly, he let his brother go and returned to his chair to allow his leg to rest.

After a few moments of unbearable silence, Bobby finally looked him in the eye. "I've thought a lot about dying. Getting out of this body."

Sawyer's tears were now freely falling from his chin and onto his shirt. His heart ached for his brother and the cards he'd been dealt. Knowing he was responsible for his brother's pain drove Sawyer near crazy.

"I'm sorry, Bobby, this is all my fault. I should be in that chair instead of you." His voice was gravelly and rough as he forced out the words. "We would've never been there that day if it wasn't for me."

Bobby's eyebrows drew together, and his expression changed to concern. "What do you mean it's your fault? That other driver was drunk."

"True, but it was me who brought us there to begin with. If we hadn't been celebrating my scholarship, none of this would have happened. Mom and dad would be alive, and you wouldn't be stuck in that chair. This is all on me."

Bobby looked at him oddly, as if seeing something for the first time. "Shit, you've thought this is all because we went out to celebrate your scholarship. That's crazy. I don't blame you, and I'm positive mom and dad wouldn't either."

"It's because you're so soft-hearted you can't see my culpability." Sawyer wouldn't allow his brother to wash away his sin so easily. "If I hadn't insisted we had to go to Pasadena for dinner, then we wouldn't have been in the car. Our lives would have gone on as usual. I took that away from you, mom and dad. How can you ever forgive me?"

Sawyer buried his head in his hands, ashamed of himself and mourning what he had caused and lost. He could picture his parents sitting in the front seat, laughing and cheering when he'd told them about the scholarship, followed almost immediately by his mother's scream and the sound of bending metal and breaking of glass.

A drunk driver had crossed the center lane and hit their car head-on doing fifty. The impact sent their car slamming into a metal light pole on Bobby's side of the car, bending the car around the pole like it was made of tin foil. They were crushed where they sat.

They never had a chance.

The electric engine on Bobby's wheelchair started up, and Sawyer wholly expected him to leave the room. He didn't want to be around himself, so he understood the feeling. Instead of leaving, Bobby came closer and laid his stiff hand on Sawyer's bowed head.

"I love you too, Sawyer," he said. "At the moment, my saying you're not responsible for what happened to us isn't going to change your mind. We both have things we need to work on."

"Yeah, we do," Sawyer agreed, raising his head to look at Bobby. "I think it's time for both of us to talk to somebody."

"You mean like therapy or something?"

"That's precisely what I mean." He'd been thinking about it for a while.

"I don't want to talk to somebody about my emotions and shit."

"I don't think we have a choice. Neither of us is happy, and we blame ourselves for different reasons. It's toxic, bro." Sawyer felt the rightness of that statement.

Bobby blamed himself for how they lived, and Sawyer blamed himself for the accident that got them there. "Please. Do it for me."

Bobby took his time and thought it over, which Sawyer appreciated. Therapy wasn't going to be easy, but at this point, what did they have to lose?

"I'll make you a deal," Bobby said, reminding Sawyer of the deal he'd made with his brother about school. "If I agree to try out therapy, you have to agree to start opening up to the idea that the accident wasn't your fault."

"But—,"

Bobby cut him off. "I know it's going to be hard. We'll start with you allowing the idea to infiltrate in that smart brain of yours until it doesn't feel so weird."

Bobby wasn't asking for more than Sawyer wanted from him. He wanted his brother to talk to someone for a long time without much success. If this were the only way to get Bobby into therapy, he'd take it.

"Fine, deal," Sawyer agreed. "Don't get your hopes up. I know what I've done."

Bobby smiled sadly and laid his forearm on Sawyer's shoulder. "We're a couple of fucked-up people."

"Ding, ding, ding. You are correct, sir. Your prize is a life staring at my sorry mug," Sawyer grumbled.

"I can handle that," Bobby said as Sawyer lowered his forehead to lean against his brother's arm.

"So can I."

# Chapter Eight

Alexander stood outside of Sawyer's temporary apartment unsure if he should knock. He'd been ordered to stay away and had managed to honor that request for three whole days. For some reason, he'd spent that time thinking about Sawyer and his brother to the point of distraction. What was wrong with him?

He'd been preoccupied with the dishwasher, and wanted to get to know him better. He'd lose track of time, and spend hours staring at his living room wall. When he was in his kitchen, he was in the zone. Nothing and no one could break his concentration. In the intervening hours, his brain got on the Sawyer train, and there were no stops. Against his better judgment, here he stood staring at the woodgrain of Sawyer's front door.

"Are you going to knock or stand there a while and think about it?" Janice asked from somewhere behind him, causing him to jump and spin around.

"Shit," he whispered, not wanting anyone inside to hear him. "Why are you sneaking up on me?"

Janice smiled wide and crossed her arms. "I wasn't sneaking anywhere. I work here, remember?"

Alexander knew he was busted. "You wouldn't accept that I'm lost, would you?"

"Not a chance." Her smile grew as she flipped her pink hair out of her face. He could have sworn it had been colored blue the last time he saw her, or was it purple?

"You know, there's a custom of knocking on doors when you want to be let in. You ever hear of it?"

"Yes, I've heard of it," Alexander huffed. "The problem is I don't know how I'll be greeted if I do."

Janice's expression changed, and she uncrossed her arms. "You're worried Sawyer won't let you in after all that's happened."

"Exactly. He asked me to stay away from him." God, he felt like a seventeen-year-old again.

"Then, why are you here?"

Good question. "Because I'm an idiot."

"Well, this I have to hear." She laughed.

Alexander ran his fingers through his rapidly greying hair while trying to decide how much to say. "I'm concerned and wanted to check in with them before I head down to the kitchen."

"So, knock," Janice dared.

"It's not that easy," he said. "Sawyer gave me the heave-ho the last time I was here."

"Yet here you stand." It was obvious she was deriving immense joy from his squirming.

"I should go," he said before turning away to go down the hall.

Suddenly, the door opened, and Sawyer stood in the doorway with the help of his walker. "I thought I heard people talking out here."

Janice jumped right in. "Alexander has come to check on you and Bobby. Invite him in." He'd met crocodiles in the Nile with more timidity than this woman.

Sawyer looked uncertain but stepped back and asked, "Would you like to come in?"

Not waiting for his reply, Janice took hold of Alexander's arm and led him inside.

"I'll make coffee. You two can go sit in the living room," Janice instructed before veering off toward the kitchen. "Sawyer, play nice."

Sawyer led the way to the living room, and soon they were sitting in chairs facing each other. Alexander didn't quite know where to start, so he decided another apology was in order. "I'm sorry."

"I'm sorry," Sawyer said at the same time. "Wait. What?"

"You're sorry for what?" Alexander asked. "You did nothing wrong."

"Neither did you," Sawyer stated.

*This is unexpected.* "I yelled at you. That's what started this whole thing." Alexander's sense of self-preservation must've left his body, or he would've accepted Sawyer's apology and called it a day.

"You were upset at the time, and I should have been more vigilant with all the wait staff running around like that. It was a busy night." Sawyer sounded too logical, and Alexander didn't like it. The man he was coming to know was full of emotion and passion.

"I brought Cooper into your life," Alexander said, trying to get his point across.

"What Cooper did was his fault, not yours," Sawyer countered, sounding a lot like Jillian.

*Not so fast.* "I forced you to have to flee your home."

"Nope, that was Cooper again. Along with the reporters' help."

"What about the insurance company?" The news must have reached them by now.

"Yeah, well, they still want to send out a stooge, and they asked the same caseworker to check out the place and to discuss what happened at the zoo." Sawyer's voice took a notable shift toward anger.

"When will they be coming?" Alexander didn't miss the stressful look that crossed Sawyer's face either.

"Next Wednesday. At least I'll have my leg brace by then," Sawyer managed a small smile, and Alexander knew it was for his benefit.

There was no way he'd let Sawyer face them alone. "I'd like you to have legal counsel with you when they come." No more games with this company.

"Bobby said he gave you access to all our paperwork. I didn't hire anyone, so I'm guessing that's you."

"It is. I spoke with my sister and father, they run the family business, and they told me a Ms. Winters would be the best person to represent the two of you. She's gone over your documents and would welcome the opportunity to represent you."

"I guess that would be okay with the insurance company," Sawyer said, striking a sour note. Clearly, Sawyer didn't understand Ms. Winters would be pursuing the insurance company for their misdeeds. The days of toeing the line for them was over, and a change in thinking was in order.

"I don't give a damn what they think or want. This is about you and Bobby and what's best for the two of you." Alexander could feel his blood boiling thinking about all the pressure the company had placed on Sawyer when he was recovering from multiple surgeries.

"If I had my way, I'd drag the fuckers to court. Excuse my language."

So far, Ms. Winter's legal team had found more than a few discrepancies between what the policy covered and what Sawyer and Bobby had received. The sad part was that Alexander wasn't shocked. Insurance policies were great until you needed to use them, and without proper counsel, most people didn't have a full grasp of their rights. Sawyer looked a bit shocked, but Alexander would be damned if he'd take back his words.

"I can't afford a lawyer."

"You don't need to. When she gets done, the insurance company will be paying her fee."

"Okay, then can you have Ms. Winters come by around nine Wednesday morning? The others will be arriving around eleven."

"She'll be here. It's a good idea for her to come out early. She has a few things she wishes to discuss with you," Alexander explained.

"Something wrong?" Sawyer's brows drew together.

"Not for you, but Ms. Winters has a few pointed questions for your insurance company. No one is ever going to take advantage of the two of you again."

Sawyer sat there for a few moments in silence, making Alexander wonder if he'd gone too far.

"Look, I treated you badly the last time you were here, and I'm sorry about that. I was caught up, and I directed all that emotion at you. Once I calmed down a bit, I began to see things more clearly, and came up with one undeniable fact. You're not responsible for any of this."

"We'll agree to disagree on that point." Alexander wasn't so ready to let himself off the hook.

"I'm guessing you're the one footing the bill for all this, and you don't have to. I don't blame you anymore for anything." Sawyer spread out to encompass the entire condo.

"Listen, the firm is on retainer, and it's no big deal. Can't a friend do something for another friend?" Okay, Alexander had to admit that was lame.

"We weren't friends before things blew up. We barely live on the same planet." Sawyer chuckled.

"You're not making this easy. It hasn't exactly been a stellar year for me," Alexander said as he rubbed the back of his neck.

"Having that psycho, Cooper, as your boyfriend is proof enough of that, but we all make mistakes. You're not responsible for my brother or me."

"I'll have you know it's been a team effort. Saint donated the condo. I covered your brace and got the legal team activated. The rest of the crew chipped in here and there when help was needed moving things and protecting you." It wasn't as if Alexander was doing all this on his own. The crew here at The Gates reminded him of a small town, looking out for one another.

"Protecting us?" Sawyer choked out.

"No. Not in a spy thriller kind of way, but keeping an eye out for any reporters who happen by." It wasn't as if they had guards at the doors or anything. However, if that big ex-marine, Miguel, had his way, they'd be inspecting identification. The man took any perceived threat to a member of the crew as a personal assault.

"Do they already know where I am?" Sawyer asked, his eyes darting from side to side as if someone was going to pop out.

"I don't think so," Alexander replied. "No one's been around, and the newspapers have been pretty silent."

"I'm surprised Cooper isn't still on his press tour."

"Well, from what I've heard, once his father got wind of what happened, Cooper was forced to return back out East to answer a few serious questions." Alexander would have loved being a fly on the wall for that conversation.

"So, Cooper's family found out anyway?" Sawyer asked while giving Alexander a knowing look.

"Yes, and it wasn't me who did it," Alexander answered with his hands up in mock surrender.

"But I bet you know who it was," Sawyer stated.

"Maybe. Either way, Cooper is no longer on the West Coast, and I don't suspect he'll cause any further harm." Thank God for that.

"Thank you. I was afraid to open a newspaper since I read that Trey guy's article the first day."

"You're welcome," Alexander said before looking around for Janice.

"If you're looking for that coffee, it's not coming." Sawyer chuckled again.

"What?"

"Janice, she's not the coffee making type. She likely wanted us to talk it out and used the guise of freshly brewed coffee to make that happen," Sawyer explained. "If she brought us anything, it'd be a wheatgrass, tree bark smoothie."

"Crafty," Alexander agreed.

"You have no idea," Sawyer said with a slow roll of his eyes. "You want her on your side."

Alexander nodded. He surmised she was formidable. "Well, I should head down to the kitchen. We're serving red wine braised duck with a warm red beet salad and mashed pumpkin as the special tonight."

"Oh, that sounds good," Sawyer said, then added, "I mean, there should be lots of people coming in to enjoy that meal."

"I agree. I'll send you, Bobby, and Janice plates so you all can try it, and you can let me know how we did." Alexander would welcome any reason to keep a personal connection to Sawyer.

"You don't have—"

"I know I'm under no obligation to do anything. We're friends now, and I like doing things for my friends. What time would be best?"

"Anytime around five, please," Sawyer said. "Bobby usually falls asleep early."

"You got it," Alexander said as he stood. "Three duck dinners up, literally."

Sawyer laughed as Alexander had hoped, and after a round of goodbyes, he was back in his kitchen, mind clear and hopes renewed.

This time his night went by without any frustrating distractions. Though Sawyer wasn't far from his thoughts, the worry had subsided, and a new friendship had begun.

From there, he could work on the rest.

# Chapter Nine

Today would mark the fourth day this week their kitchen had been commandeered, and Sawyer was beginning to wonder if they had a new roommate. Not that he minded, the view was nothing scoff at.

Dressed in a faded t-shirt and worn jeans molded to his thick thighs and a perfect ass, Alexander moved around the kitchen. Sawyer couldn't help but watch the chef's muscles flex as his body flowed gracefully from one pan or appliance to another. The man was an artist with food. There was no other way to describe how he cooked. His passion was unmistakable and downright distracting.

After sending the tender duck with its crispy skin upstairs for them to try earlier in the week, Alexander was now in the habit of showing up to create the nightly special for Sawyer, Bobby, and Janice. He fit it in between his morning prep and returning downstairs to supervise the dinner service in his real kitchen.

The chef never really asked permission, but then again, Sawyer didn't argue.

"You enjoying what you're reading?" Bobby asked as he wheeled up beside Sawyer's chair in the living room. He loved open concept living. No matter where he sat, Sawyer could still see Alexander. It was an inescapable bonus of this condo.

Sawyer looked down at the borrowed laptop to do a bit of research into Cal State Fullerton campus distance learning options, to find the screen had timed out, leaving a lush tropical landscape screen saver in its place. How long had he been sitting there like that?

He quickly shut the laptop before answering his brother. "I was lost in thought, that's all."

"I can tell you exactly where those thoughts were centered," Bobby said with a wiggle of his eyebrows. "Can't blame you, though."

Sawyer turned to look at his brother. He'd never mentioned being attracted to anyone before.

"What?" Bobby asked, looking back at him. "I can appreciate a perfect example of the male form as much as a female's."

"You've got me there," Sawyer answered truthfully as Janice came around the corner carrying Bobby's jacket. "Where are you two off to?" He wasn't sure he wanted his brother out in the world yet, even though there hadn't been a word written in the tabloids since Cooper's initial interview.

"We're blowing this popsicle stand, man. Hitting the road, pounding the pavement," Bobby declared. "I need fresh air, bro. You should come with us. We'll be back before dinner."

Sawyer wasn't quite ready to put his face out there for everyone to see. He was probably overreacting and accepted that. "No. You guys go. Be careful while you're out, please."

Janice looked Sawyer straight in the eyes with that laser focus of hers. "They'd have to get past me to get near him."

While Sawyer appreciated the reassurance, Bobby went with his typical banter. "Look, I have a bodyguard. I wouldn't mess with her."

Janice flexed her tattooed arms showing off a whole lot more muscle than Sawyer ever suspected she had under those loose scrubs. It took a lot of strength to take care of people with mobility issues. Transfers required her to lift Bobby repeated from one spot to another, like the bath or his work-out mat. Sawyer had a hell of a lot of respect for PSW's and nurses.

"Neither would I," Sawyer agreed. Janice would protect Bobby, and he knew it. "Have fun."

"We'll be back soon. If you're not coming along, don't waste time sitting here alone," Bobby whispered while Janice slipped on his jacket.

"Waste what?" Sawyer never wasted time. There was always one thing or another to do.

"Your alone time with the hunky chef who can't stop himself from needing to be near you," Janice explained as if Sawyer was a brick short of a load.

"Near me? You've got it wrong. Alexander feels guilty. That's what this is. I tried to tell him it wasn't his fault, but he refused to listen to me, so now we have a cook." And Sawyer thought he was the one with the wild imagination in this family.

"Believe what you want to believe, but don't throw the possibility away without first making sure," Bobby said, then winked. "We'll be about forty minutes."

Sawyer watched as the two stopped to speak with Alexander before heading out of the door. The chef's smile widened before he went back to this evening's masterpiece. Sawyer had no idea what the hell those two meant by their comment. Alexander had shown up only after the zoo incident. His guilt was forcing him to come by every day and check-in.

*Then why is he cooking for you?* Sawyer hated that little voice in his head. They argued incessantly.

Because he likes to cook.

*Oh, c'mon, you're kidding yourself. You've been off the playing field for too long.*

Alexander wanted nothing to do with the train wreck that was Sawyer. Once things quieted down, Alexander would return to his life, and Bobby and Sawyer would return to theirs. He and the chef didn't exactly run in the same circles, so it wouldn't take long before Alexander was distracted by something or someone else and forgot about Sawyer's little family.

That stung, and it hadn't even happened yet.

Using his walker, Sawyer stood and turned toward the kitchen to join the cause of his distraction and confusion. He'd get to the bottom of this. He'd prove to his brother and Janice that they lived in a dream world where handsome, rich, accomplished, eligible men were attracted to average, poor, disabled men.

Alexander smiled when he noticed Sawyer limping toward the kitchen island. "Coming to help with dinner?"

"Sure, what do you need me to do?" He might as well help.

"Would you mind slicing the strawberries for my fruit compote that's going over the vanilla bean ice cream?" Alexander asked while holding up a box of fresh strawberries.

"No problem." Sawyer climbed onto one of the barstools surrounding the marble island. There were different widths, and where he sat, there wasn't a wide slab separating him from Alexander.

Along with Alexander's attention, Sawyer was careful not to get too used to this condo's upscale amenities, like double ovens and all the burners working on the stovetop at the same time. This was temporary. "Set me up."

Alexander brought over a cutting board, knife, and a box of strawberries along with a bowl. "Here you go, and I won't say a word if a few berries were to disappear," he said with a conspiratorial wink that raised Sawyer's heart rate.

Okay, they were friends. Friends did things like that. Nothing unusual. *Right?*

To draw Alexander's attention away from him, Sawyer said, "I can see the steaks ready for the grill. What fancy meal do we have today?'

"We're having grilled New York strip steak with *smashed* garlic potatoes and sautéed green beans. I went simple tonight because it's my night off." Another wink. Maybe he had something in his eye.

*You're hopeless.*

Sawyer dropped the knife onto the cutting board. "It's your night off. What the hell are you doing here then? I thought you were swinging by before going back downstairs like always. You didn't have to come here to cook for us. I'm sure there are a million other things you'd want to be doing with your night off."

"Nope, this is about perfect. I brought along a few movies we could choose from after dinner if you're into it," Alexander suggested nonchalantly.

"Wow, dinner and a movie. You know how to sweep a guy off his feet," Sawyer teased and went back to cutting the berries. Hell, if he wanted to hang out, he was more than welcome to join the three of them. It would be fun for Bobby to have a movie night.

Sawyer looked up from his duties at the sound of that telltale sizzle. The steaks were on. He finished with the berries, and Alexander gathered them into a smaller pot before placing it on the stove. He added honey, spices, and lemon juice to the mixture and stirred it before returning to the steaks.

The smashed potatoes were roasting in the oven, and the green beans were sautéing in another pan. The entire condo was filled with mouth-watering scents and the homey sounds of pots and pans. For a moment, Sawyer was transported back to a time when life was good, and the world was fair. His parents were alive, and Bobby was an energetic teenager annoying the hell out of everybody.

His mom would cook dinner in the kitchen while dad watched the early news from his chair in the living room. The same chair Sawyer had been sleeping in the last few years. Their old apartment wasn't anything special, but it had always felt perfect. Warm and inviting, filled with love, laughter, and people. Lots of people.

Other residents would stop by for coffee and to sit and talk. It wasn't odd to come home and find neighbors in the kitchen laughing and talking up a storm with his parents. He remembered thinking the place was crowded at the time. Now he'd give anything to be stuck in the middle of that kitchen again.

"Sawyer, hey, are you okay?" Alexander's voice penetrated Sawyer's memories, and the images quickly faded away. "Do you need anything?"

When he refocused, Sawyer realized the chef was leaning over the kitchen island and was only inches from his face. He couldn't move as he cataloged the dark blue flecks in Alexander's light blue eyes. They were stunning.

"Are you with me, Sawyer?" Alexander asked.

"Yeah." His voice came out throaty and deeper than normal.

"You scared me when you didn't answer me before. Are you sure you're good?" Alexander looked legitimately concerned.

"I was caught in a memory," Sawyer explained. Neither of them had moved away.

"A good one, I hope."

"A time before the car accident. Your cooking reminded me of home."

"I can't think of a better compliment." Alexander's voice took on a deeper tone.

"It's true." Sawyer didn't want him to think he was bullshitting.

He wasn't sure if he or Alexander had moved to close the distance between them. Sawyer could almost touch the stubble on Alexander's chiseled jaw. He should be pulling away, he shouldn't even be contemplating kissing the handsome man, but dammit he was.

Alexander's warm breath fanned against Sawyer's lips inviting him to taste until there was no other choice, and for the first time since the accident, Sawyer thought of himself first and took what he wanted.

Their lips met, and Sawyer was surprised by how soft Alexander's lips were. He chased the sweet taste of honey from the compote and dove in for more, feeling out of control. He wondered if those moans were his or Alexander's.

Sawyer had never been kissed so thoroughly as Alexander's tongue explored, only stopping when he nibbled on Sawyer's lips and jaw. It felt as if his world was spinning, and he held tight to Alexander's strong arms as his chef held him in place.

Before Sawyer attempted to crawl over the island, bum leg and all, to get a better hold on the sexy man, they heard that unmistakable sound of the lock snicking open. They broke apart so quickly that Sawyer almost missed his seat when he tried to sit back down. If it weren't for Alexander's hold, Sawyer would've been sprawled on the tiled floor.

He grabbed a nearby magazine and hoped he could hide his flushed face behind it because there was no chance of standing to leave with the hard-on he was sporting. Alexander gave him a cheeky grin before adjusting his apron and returning to the grill top to flip the steaks.

The front door opened wide, allowing Bobby to roll in first. Janice followed, cradling something in her arms.

"Look what Finn gave me," Bobby yelled as he wheeled closer to the island. Janice joined them and held out a small puff of black fur with big green eyes and a tail.

"A cat. I thought we talked about how big of a responsibility a pet would be." With working and taking care of Bobby, Sawyer didn't have time to care for an animal.

"Cats are low maintenance. Feed them and clean their litter box. That's about it. There aren't any walks involved, and she came with the fixings," Booby said, and Janice held up a plastic bag as proof.

"Where did Finn find a kitten?" Alexander asked, bringing Sawyer's attention back to the sexy man. Forbidden fruit.

"His cat, Velcro, had a litter, and Oscar here needed a home. I thought he'd fit in great with us." Bobby was working hard to sell this.

"You named him Oscar?" Sawyer asked.

"Yeah," Bobby answered with a lift of his chin, daring Sawyer to deny him this.

That had been the name of their mom's cat, who'd died of old age before the accident. Well, shit. His hands were tied.

"Do we even have kitty litter?" Sawyer acquiesced.

Both Bobby and Janice smiled, knowing full well he'd give in. "Finn said it's in the bag. We need to sacrifice something to put it in."

"Would this do?" Alexander asked as he raised a large rectangular plastic container from the cupboard. It was only a couple of inches tall, so the kitten should be able to climb over it to do his business.

"That's perfect," Bobby said, and Janice placed the kitten on his brother's lap while pulling the items out of the bag. Sure enough, there was a small bag of litter, cans of kitten food, and toys for the little puffball.

Sawyer watched as Oscar curled up on Bobby's lap, making himself comfortable instead of trying to get away or climb his brother like a tree. "Fine, Oscar can stay. He can join our little bubble of bachelors and bachelorette."

"Thank you," Bobby said while brushing his stiff fingers over the kitten's fur. "So what'd you guys get up to while we were gone?"

Sawyer looked at Alexander, who was already staring at him with that damn grin of his. "I was helping Alexander with dinner, and it's almost ready, so you two better go get Oscar settled while I set the table."

Without waiting for a reply, Sawyer reached for his walker and finally was able to stand now that another part of his body had calmed down.

How could he explain what happened when Sawyer wasn't even sure himself?

This was going to be one hell of a dinner and movie night.

*** 

Alexander watched Sawyer squirm. He was avoiding eye contact and was so damned adorable doing it.

Alexander was certain of the simmering attraction between them. The moment their lips touched, the attraction was confirmed and ratcheted up several heat levels, from a simmer to a low boil.

How could he not be attracted to him? Sawyer embodied everything Alexander had ever wanted in a man and was sexy as hell. If for no other reason than the way Sawyer was with his brother, the strength of his character shone like a beacon. His leg concerned Alexander only because of the pain it caused Sawyer, which reminded him. He wanted to talk to Sawyer about his options. There were so many new therapies for repairing structural and tissue damage. Alexander had to sit him down and have "the talk."

"This is fabulous," Janice moaned after having her first bite of steak. "I swear you have a magic touch."

Sawyer began coughing as he tried to place his glass of water down in front of his plate.

"You okay, bro?" Bobby asked from the other side of the table.

"Yeah," Sawyer gasped. "Water went down the wrong pipe."

"Thank you," Alexander said to Janice. He knew he would catch hell for this, but he couldn't help it. "Sawyer. You think I have a magic touch?"

The man's fork clattered off the table and onto the floor. When Sawyer bent down to pick it up, he shot Alexander a look that should have scorched him, but all he could do was smile. He hadn't had this much fun in a while. In fact, the last several days had been some of his happiest since moving to the West coast.

Sawyer sat up and said without a hint of anger he'd sent through that laser glare, "Could be a magic touch but don't discount top-notch ingredients and a fully stocked kitchen of gadgets that helped prepare it. It takes more than magic to make something work."

Despite the confused looks on both Bobby and Janice's faces, Alexander was up for the challenge. "So, you're saying that my abilities alone aren't everything."

"Well, yeah. There are many things to consider when putting a *dish* together. Like the hardworking farmers who sowed the seeds for these vegetables, and the people who bring it to market, and everyone in between."

"I understand and appreciate all the hard work that has gone into providing excellent ingredients." Alexander didn't know if Sawyer was jabbing him or making a point beyond the surface discussion. It wasn't lost on him that the economic hardships Sawyer and his brother face every day made them closer to the realities of life for every working person.

"Without one, there isn't the other," Sawyer shot back.

"Understood." There was no food on the table without Sawyer, and there was no Sawyer without Bobby.

"Huh?" Janice said as she and Bobby stared at the two of them. "They already got a secret language. Damn, that was fast."

Sawyer dug into his dinner, signaling the end of the conversation. When they were done, Janice offered to clean up while the three went into the living room to set up for movie night. Alexander had brought the DVDs along in hopes of gaining more time with Sawyer. Jillian had flown home to keep an eye on Cooper and her ear to the ground for press stirrings.

Her vigilance was necessary. Cooper was capable of all sorts of heinous acts and behavior. Surveillance was a must until something or someone else came along to take his attention away from Sawyer. It was like dealing with a toddler. A spoiled, rich, pissed off, petulant toddler who no one ever reined in.

"Whatcha bring?" Bobby asked as he positioned his chair in front of the couch. "An action movie?"

Alexander dumped the bag with the DVDs onto the coffee table so Bobby could choose. "I've got *Spider-Man: Into the Spider-Verse, Black Panther, Star Wars: The Force Awakens,* and *Rise of Skywalker, Wonder Woman,* and *Captain Marvel.*"

"You're into the franchises, huh?" Sawyer quipped.

"I know. I'm a geek. But Marvel and *Star Wars*, how can you beat them for action and adventure?" Alexander asked.

"You and I are going to get along just fine," Bobby said, which made Sawyer smile even though he hadn't looked in Alexander's direction since he began eating.

"Okay, you can pick one movie to watch," Sawyer said, coming to sit behind his brother on the couch. "It's already past five, and you know how wiped out you are the next day if you stay up too late."

"Fine, *Captain Marvel* it is," Bobby announced. "I'm all for women kicking ass."

"Damn straight," Janice yelled from the kitchen, making all three men laugh.

Alexander joined Sawyer on the couch, much to his surprise. This whole dynamic was new and had him off balance. Usually, when Alexander met someone he wanted to date, he would wine and dine them. Food was his go-to. This time, he knew he'd have to work harder than ever before.

Sawyer was worth whatever it took.

# Chapter Ten

Sawyer didn't know what the hell he was thinking when he kissed Alexander. It had been a spur of the moment decision. No. Actually, that wasn't right. He'd had no choice but to kiss him. He'd been pulled to him. That kiss had blown the doors off his resolve to keep the chef at arm's length. Regretting the kiss: nah. Regretting the impossibility of their situation: yep.

Annoyingly, the guy was sitting a foot away on the couch, grinning like a damn cat.

Speaking of cats, Oscar was curled up on Bobby's lap, purring away. His brother's arm lay protectively beside his new BF to make sure he didn't roll off. Sawyer wasn't sure how the furball got up there, but he didn't like the thought of it climbing his brother's leg to do it. That Bobby couldn't feel those tiny nails poking his into skin didn't make it okay.

"We'll have to come up with something to help Oscar climb up your chair," Sawyer said as he got up, grabbed his walker, and limped over to slide the DVD into the machine to start the movie.

When he turned around, he saw Alexander on his knees in front of Bobby, inspecting the side of his chair. "I have an idea. We can get a thin scratching post and attach the vertical part to the side of your chair. The cat can climb up using that without scratching your legs."

"Sounds perfect," Bobby agreed. "Where's the nearest pet store?"

Leave it to a seventeen-year-old to expect instant gratification. Most of the time, his brother seemed older than his years. When the excited teenager came out, Sawyer loved it.

"How about I pick one up for you and Oscar on my way over tomorrow? Then Sawyer and I can put it on," Alexander suggested.

"What time are you coming over?" Bobby asked, his impatience showing.

"Yeah, what time?" Sawyer repeated, only realizing afterward that his voice made it sound like he was looking forward to seeing him. "I mean, since you always feel the need to drop in anyway, it'd be nice to have an ETA."

And there it was, that damn smile. Why did Alexander have to look so good when Sawyer was trying to snarky?

"Around ten," he replied. "Hey, isn't Monday the day you get your new brace?"

"That's what the Orthotist's office told me."

"Great. I can't wait to see how it fits."

"Okay, let's get this show on the road, boys," Janice announced as she joined them in the living room. "I figured we'd have our dessert out here." She raised a tray holding four bowls of ice cream and Alexander's fruit compote.

At the sight of the dessert, Sawyer's face warmed. Instead of grabbing a bowl, he went back to the couch the moment his cock began to twitch from heated memories of *that kiss*. It'd been a long time since Sawyer had given any thought to his own needs and wants, but his body remembered what it wanted.

One strategically placed throw pillow later, and he was ensconced on the couch.

"Here you go," Alexander said, and Sawyer looked up to find him holding two bowls of ice cream covered in sweet, fruity goodness. He was doomed. "You forgot your dessert."

Thankfully, Janice was there to help Bobby with his bowl because Sawyer couldn't move. He took the offered bowl and spoon and growled out, "Thank you."

"You're welcome," Alexander said, looking as innocent as an angel. Sawyer knew by the glint in his eyes the chef was baiting him.

Payback was sharpening her claws, and he didn't think of the consequences. Since Bobby and Janice were sitting slightly in front of the couch, Sawyer was out of their view. He dipped the tip of the spoon into the compote and brought it to his mouth, stuck out his tongue, and cleaned the spoon, making sure it was licked clean before diving in for more.

Sawyer glanced at Alexander, who didn't look so cocky anymore: his mouth was hanging open. Next scoop held a good portion of ice cream, and Sawyer licked his lips suggestively before moving onto stage two: the suck. He put the entire spoonful of ice cream in his mouth and then slowly pulled the spoon out, leaving a portion of the ice cream on the spoon. Each time he sucked it back in, it came out with a little less ice cream.

By now, Alexander was laser-focused on Sawyer's lips, as intended. With another spoonful, Sawyer gave it the same thorough treatment eliciting a soft moan, which was drowned out by the explosions coming from the television. When Sawyer felt his chef was all in, he bit down on the remaining portion of ice cream, then sucked it back.

Alexander began coughing, his face turning a deep shade of red. He said, "Excuse me," before getting up and heading for the guest bathroom on the other side of the kitchen.

Both Bobby and Janice turned to look at Sawyer with questioning gazes. He shrugged and said, "Must've choked on the ice cream."

Janice smiled evilly and pointed off to the corner of the room. Sawyer turned to look and found a mirror hanging above the desk that provided them with a perfect view of him and Alexander. *Shit.* This time it was Sawyer who was turning red.

"You're playing with fire with that one," Janice warned.

Bobby looked at him with his face all scrunched up like he smelled something bad. "Eww, bro. Keep that shit behind closed doors."

"Weren't you the two who told me not to waste time?"

"We said to get to know him, not to use dessert as a phallic replacement." Janice laughed.

"Do you always have to be an overachiever?" Bobby asked with a smile. "But seriously, keep it in the bedroom, man."

Sawyer laid his head back on the couch and stared at the ceiling. Story of his life. Just when he thinks he has the upper hand, the tables are turned, and he's busted down again.

"It'll never work anyway," he mumbled.

"What won't work?" Alexander asked as he sat back down beside Sawyer.

Janice said without missing a beat, "Bobby watching *Star Wars* after this movie."

"Gotta agree. Both movies are over two hours long. You'd be getting to bed way late."

Bobby seemed to be thinking it over. Was his brother always this good at acting? "Okay, but maybe we can watch it tomorrow night."

"Sounds like a deal, buddy," Alexander said, and Bobby smiled huge. Their dad used to call his brother *buddy* all the time.

Sawyer turned his attention to the movie and finished his ice cream minus the sideshow. Sometime later, he felt a breeze on his face and looked up to find Alexander laying the throw blanket over him. How'd he know Sawyer was getting cold?

When Alexander sat down, he didn't pull the blanket on him, surprising Sawyer. He thought for sure the chef would want to get under there. Maybe Sawyer had pushed too far with the ice-cream stunt. Moments later, the chef found Sawyer's hand, entangled their fingers, and held on tight.

That was more like it.

***

It seemed the evenings were getting colder faster this year, and he zipped up his flimsy jacket. Standing here like an idiot waiting was beginning to feel like being put on bullshit duty. So far, he'd seen the brother, Bobby, come out of The Gates confirming that Sawyer was in that building somewhere. Now he simply had to figure out how to get in there, which might be more difficult than he'd first imagined.

A guy, the size of a house, was never far from the entrance. Had to be security. There was nothing in his job description about taking on the big guy, and he would avoid doing so at all cost.

There had to be another way into the building, and he'd better find it soon because pictures of the mark's brother wouldn't make his new client happy.

He had to get concrete proof before a move was made, or he'd be fired. So here he sat day after day, waiting for a glimpse of some guy. Even though the pay was generous, it still sucked. Times were hard, and he had to accept the contract for this cat and mouse bullshit.

*Where are you, Sawyer Hudson?*

# Chapter Eleven

Monday morning dawned bright and early. Sawyer wanted to be ready for the Orthotist. Typically, he didn't look forward to things happening anymore since, more times than not; he was disappointed. Not this time. A new brace would allow him to have his mobility back, and that's what he needed before he could return to work. Washing dishes with his walker... Ah, no.

He was about to start preparing breakfast when he heard a soft meow. He looked down to find Oscar staring up at him with those brilliant emerald eyes.

"I suppose you're hungry." He reached down and picked up the fluffball, and it immediately began purring. "Save those purrs for Bobby, runt." He had nothing against the cat, but he'd prefer it to bond with Bobby because that's what would make his brother happiest.

Sawyer picked up one of the tins of food on the counter and opened it. One look inside made him wonder how expensive this stuff was because it looked like a miniature stew, beef chunks and all. Was that a pea?

"Shit, you're eating better than I did." At least before coming here to The Gates. Now he had his own chef. Sort of.

He placed a bowl full of cat food and another with water on the counter and sat the puffball beside it. Sawyer figured Oscar would be safer high up and wouldn't get run over with his walker.

Grabbing the carton of eggs and brick of cheddar from the refrigerator, Sawyer went about making cheesy omelets for Janice, Bobby, and himself. They were Bobby's favorite breakfast food.

The eggs were almost ready when he heard his brother's wheelchair's motor coming from down the hall. He looked up, and sure enough, Bobby and Janice were heading to the breakfast bar attached to the kitchen island.

"'Mornin', bro," Bobby said. "What's for breakfast?'

"Your favorite, of course." Sawyer laughed.

"Yessssssss," he hissed happily.

"So, today's the big day," Janice said as she took a seat beside Bobby. "Excited?"

Sawyer began dishing out the cheesy goodness onto their plates. Grateful the larger kitchen provided ample room for his walker; he negotiated the space without tripping over himself. "Yeah. I can't wait to get back to work."

"You sure that's a good idea considering we're still not out of the woods yet with the insurance company and the caseworker?" Janice asked.

"I wish I was eighteen already so that I could lose the caseworker. I'll be considered an adult, and this crap would be over," Bobby grumbled.

"That's another six months away, but I agree. Let's get through their Wednesday visit, and if we're lucky, we won't have to see either of them again before your birthday." They'd be celebrating that day for multiple reasons.

"Here, here," Janice agreed with a lift of her glass of orange juice.

Impatient meows were being sent from behind them.

"I'll get him," Janice said as she stood and walked over to the other counter. She picked up the kitten and brought it over to Bobby. "I think he's going to be a mouthy one."

Sawyer watched as Oscar headed straight back to his spot on Bobby's lap to curl up. "Well, then he already fits in around here."

After a shared laugh, silence ensued, and everyone tucked into their meals. Sawyer wasn't a chef, but he thought he did a decent job, and by the empty plates, he figured his family did too.

Janice was helping Sawyer clear the plates when they heard a knock on their front door. His heart began to pound.

"I'll get it," Sawyer said, too excited to wait. His new leg brace was here.

He turned the handle and opened the door wide, and sure enough, the Orthotist, Katie, was standing in the hallway holding a long duffle bag in her arms. The only shock was seeing Alexander standing behind her.

"Good morning," she said. "Your new brace has arrived."

"I come bearing gifts as well," Alexander joked while holding up a large paper bag in one hand and a case in the other.

Sawyer was caught in those happy blue eyes and couldn't look away. His emotions were whirling way too fast to be normal, especially since the accident. He'd learned there were amazing people who wanted to help and horrible people who lived their lives to put up obstacles. Mostly, he kept to himself and used his emotional energy for Bobby, who needed it.

"Aren't you going to invite them in?" Bobby asked from the living room.

"Shit, sorry. Please, come in."

Alexander smiled, and Sawyer wondered if the chef was feeling the same emotions.

Sawyer led them into the living room to get a look at his new brace and his return to freedom.

"Everything came together beautifully," Katie said while unzipping the canvas bag. "I feel certain you're going to feel a big difference compared to your old brace."

Sawyer would have been jumping up and down with excitement if he could, and if it didn't make him look like a dork. When she unzipped the bag and pulled out the flat black brace, he could feel tears getting ready to run down his cheeks, but he pushed them back, not wanting to make a fool of himself.

The brace was made of sleek metal that would stabilize the hip, knee, ankle, and foot of his weaker damaged right leg. The harness that would mold around his thigh was made of plastics, while the knee and ankle joints were made of metal. The calf restraint and footplate looked to be about half the size of his old one. Where his original brace was clunky and frustrating, this new one was streamlined and less intrusive.

"Are you sure it's going to be able to hold me up?"

"You bet it will, and it's thin enough to wear under your jeans."

"I don't have to wear it on top anymore?" It wasn't that he was vain, but people tended to look at his brace and assume he wasn't a whole man. Maybe that was his perception. Yet another thing to talk to a therapist about.

"No. It'll only be visible if you're wearing shorts," Katie assured.

With the extent of damage done and the remnants of all the surgeries, he had no intention of wearing shorts again.

"Do you want to try it on?" Alexander asked, looking as excited as Sawyer felt.

"Yeah."

"Lead the way, and I'll get you all set up," Katie said. "I want to make sure every part fits properly and doesn't cause you any pain."

Sawyer led Katie to his bedroom in order to remove his jeans and try on his new brace. His heart was racing with excitement. The days of being forced to use a walker brought back painful memories for Sawyer he'd sooner forget.

Once his brace was on, he'd be one step closer to returning to the life he and Bobby had before the zoo incident. For the first time in what felt like forever, Sawyer had more than his brother to think about. He wanted to be selfish and keep Alexander for himself, no matter how illogical that sounded.

*\*\**

"So whatcha got in the bag?" Bobby asked as he brought his wheelchair closer to Alexander, who couldn't help but smile at the sight of the little black kitten curled up on Bobby's lap being ferried around like a king.

"I see Oscar has claimed his spot," Alexander said with a chuckle, making Bobby smile. "I stopped off at a pet store on my way over and picked up a few things for the new family member." He pulled out a scratching post to be modified to fit on the side of the wheelchair, a few feathered toys he couldn't resist, and a small fleece-lined cat bed. "I figured you might want a place for Oscar to sleep when you're sleeping, maybe the foot of your bed."

"Look, Oscar, you have your own bed," Bobby cooed at the little ball of fluff. Oscar raised his tiny head and rubbed the side of his face against Bobby's arm. The little bugger was a keeper.

Janice came over and picked up the bed. "I'll go put this on your bed."

The moment she was out of sight, Bobby turned a shrewd eye on Alexander. "What are your intentions with my brother?"

Alexander wasn't surprised. Bobby had no problem laying into him when he was a stranger, castigating him for yelling at his brother. He sat in a nearby chair and looked Bobby in the eye. "I want to date your brother."

"It's not just about sex?" Bobby asked straight out. "You know, he's not a toy you can throw away after you're done playing with him."

"Of course not. There's more going on here. I care for Sawyer. I'm trying to figure out how to show him in a way he'll believe me."

"Have you thought of telling him?" Leave it to Bobby to hit at the heart of the matter.

"I'm not so good with words. Never have been. I thought by showing him how much I care by helping out and cooking delicious meals would help."

"Okay, so you're more of a show your affection by doing things kind of guy."

"Exactly."

"Don't you think this is kinda fast?"

Alexander shrugged. "This time together has allowed me the opportunity to get to know him. I don't think it's too fast. We're friends learning about each other."

"And if you two work out and move in together, what happens to me?" Bobby asked.

"You move in too," Alexander stated, knowing it was a forgone conclusion. He hoped Bobby believed it.

"Really?" Bobby looked a bit stunned. "You don't have to think about it? My brother and I come with a lot of baggage. Parents died in a horrible crash, two sons forever changed, one riddled with guilt blaming himself for the accident."

Alexander was surprised to hear that. "You'd move in. There's no way this works without you. You and Sawyer are a package deal, and I'm happy about that. Sawyer would be lost without you." Which was true, and Alexander cared for Bobby as a brother would. "Now, are we talking about Sawyer believing he's the cause of the accident?"

"Yeah," Bobby said. "You can't cut and run if this gets too real for you."

"I understand," Alexander agreed. "That's not my MO."

"Please don't break his heart," Bobby pleaded. "You'll never find a better person."

"I learning that. I don't intend to hurt Sawyer, but sometimes things happen in relationships. I'm sure you remember your parents fighting from time to time."

As Bobby nodded, their conversation was cut short when he heard Sawyer's bedroom door opening. Alexander stood to see Sawyer's expression. That would be the best way to judge his response to his new brace. Katie came out first with a big smile. He'd chosen her for this job because of the amazing work she'd done for one of his family's charities. So far, with her help and countless others, they'd been able to provide mobility aids to thousands of underprivileged children across America.

When Sawyer emerged, he looked ready to burst with excitement. He was on his own two feet again. Sawyer walked into the living room with a limp, but he looked steady. Alexander could make out only a few places where Sawyer's brace was noticeable, and by the speed, he walked it appeared to fit him perfectly.

He stopped a few feet away from Alexander. "It's… It's so light and molds around my leg like a glove. I never knew that was possible. Instead of feeling jerky around the joints, the brace glides smoothly, and I barely notice the footplate inside my shoe. I don't even want to try to imagine what something this advanced cost. To me, it's worth all the gold in the world."

Alexander tried to control the emotions welling up inside him. To be a part of this moment meant the world to him. "I want you to be happy."

Sawyer gave him a strange look. "You honestly do, don't you?"

"Yes."

Then Sawyer did something Alexander hadn't expected; he closed the distance between them and walked forward. Alexander opened his arms and lowered his head to rest it against Sawyer's.

"What'd I miss?" Janice asked.

"Sawyer is happy," Bobby said with a smile.

\*\*\*

A half hour later, Katie said her goodbyes after doing a thorough examination of the brace's fit and a few minor adjustments to the knee joint. Bobby's wheelchair had been fitted with a scratching post for Oscar, and Sawyer was still on a high and had yet to sit down. It felt as if he were trying to make up for the lost time. He'd never felt more stable and pain-free as he did now. This was a miracle brace.

Joey had stopped in a few minutes ago, and he and Bobby were in his brother's room playing video games. Sawyer could hear them trash-talking and laughing. Janice took the opportunity to go to her apartment.

Upon seeing Oscar, Joey made a quick call to Finn to check if Velcro had any more kittens that needed good homes. Sawyer was almost certain that Sam, Joey's boyfriend and the LAPD officer who'd gone along to make his brother feel safer when Sawyer had been incapacitated, would find he had a new family member by the end of the day.

This whole pet thing was contagious.

"Are you going to sit down anytime soon?" Alexander asked from the stove where he was busy making chicken soup. Christmas parties would be in full swing for the remainder of December, and there was a special event booked for later in the day. Alexander shouldn't be here. He had enough to do downstairs. Thankfully, the soup would last all day, along with the fresh bread he'd baked.

"I feel so light. When I walked before, it felt as though I was lifting dead weight. Don't get me wrong, the old brace kept me upright, but this feels like it's walking along with me," Sawyer said while waving his hands around his right leg for emphasis. "It's hard to explain, but the difference is mind-blowing."

"I'm so happy for you," Alexander said, his emotions shining bright from his blue eyes.

"We have a lot to discuss," Sawyer began. "My life isn't simple, you know. It'll be no walk in the park being with me."

Alexander smiled wide. "Duly noted."

"And, of course, my brother is my top priority."

"Wouldn't want it any other way."

"I'm going to start counseling to work on a few issues." Alexander might as well know how messed up Sawyer was. If the chef was going to cut and run, now was better than later.

"If you ever need an ear, I'm right here and ready."

"I don't want your money." Although, he imagined several people might see it that way.

"Neither do I."

"What?"

"My family may be rich, but we use that money to help countless others through our foundations and charities. The money isn't mine. I'm simply its caretaker."

"Like the California condors at the zoo?" Sawyer asked.

"Yes, exactly."

"Katie had mentioned working with you before on some sort of charity event." Katie turned out to be a nice person as well as a skilled Orthotist.

"Ah-huh. We provide assistive devices to underprivileged youths. Katie is one of the Orthotists who donates her time helping us do that."

"You're too perfect. What's wrong with you?"

Alexander laughed and set the ladle down on the spoon rest before saying, "I'm not perfect. Exhibit A: Cooper. I tend to get so focused on food and my work that people in my life feel shut out. My family tells me I'm bullheaded and stubborn, which, I'm sorry to say, you already know. I'm a geek with a fondness for superheroes, and you know that too."

Sawyer couldn't help but laugh. "Don't worry about geeking out around us. If money were no object, I'd take Bobby to San Diego Comic-Con. You've got nothing on him. The Garnet's next door let us borrow their laptop every so often so I could show Bobby videos from Comic-Cons around the world."

"You haven't seen my collection yet," Alexander countered with a grin. "Maybe I could show you sometime."

"Is that code for come up for a nightcap?"

Alexander's blue eyes went wide. "No. That offer has nothing to do with sex."

"Damn." Sawyer laughed as he moved closer to Alexander. "Can't fault a guy for trying." He stopped and leaned over the bubbling pot. "Your chicken soup smells amazing."

Alexander looked unsure of his next move, so Sawyer decided to help him along. He stood straight and said, "I'd like a redo of the other day before we were interrupted."

The chef didn't wait a moment longer, dove in, and took Sawyer in his arms. Their tongues and mouths explored more leisurely this time, allowing them to get a feel for each other. At least until Alexander backed him up and pinned him against the kitchen's tiled wall.

Sawyer's chef always tasted like some exotic spice or flavor, and he wanted more. Every touch and taste drove home the fact that he wanted this amazing man in his bed.

"Um… This is new," Joey said from somewhere behind them.

"Can't catch a break," Alexander mumbled into Sawyer's mouth. They broke apart to find both Joey and Bobby staring at them.

"Nah. They've been like this for days," Bobby said. "If you two are done sucking face, I wanted to tell you I'm going down to the first floor to Joey's place."

Sawyer had a big brother moment. On the one hand, he was excited his brother had a friend to do things with, and on the other, he was afraid he wouldn't be there if anything should happen.

"You have my cell number, right?" Sawyer had invested in a cheap phone that still flipped open for Bobby. He reloaded it with minutes every paycheck.

"Yeah, grandma. I have all your information, Bobby scowled.

"I'll call if anything comes up," Joey said. "Sam is home, and we won't be too long. I wanted to show Bobby our video game collection. Sam loves racing games."

"Okay, have fun, guys," Sawyer said, making his brother smile wide. "But keep track of Oscar and stay off the ground floor, okay?"

"Thanks, bro. Be back soon."

As the two went out of the front door, Alexander's cell began buzzing. He pulled it out and looked at the screen. "Shit, I have to get down to the kitchen. An order came in with twice the amount of tenderloin and half of the chicken." He pulled Sawyer back into his arms and said, "I'm sorry."

Sawyer understood. "Don't worry. We'll pick this up where we left off next time."

"Thanks for understanding," Alexander said before kissing him deeply.

Moments later, Sawyer was alone. This was the first time he'd been alone since this whole episode began. It felt strange. Aimlessly, he walked through the quiet condo and began noticing a few things of Alexander's.

His navy-blue jacket lay across the back of one of the barstools. His toolbox from this morning's wheelchair customization sat on the floor in the living room, and his faded t-shirt stuck out of his canvas gym bag sitting on the floor. Sawyer reached down to touch the fabric but came away, holding the shirt up in his hands.

He felt creepy as hell, but he brought the fabric up to his nose and was enveloped in the scent of Alexander's cologne mixed with barbeque and was transported to last night and their first kiss. Alexander had been grilling steaks for dinner.

Sawyer took another look at the shirt before folding it neatly and placing it back into Alexander's bag. His touches were everywhere. From the new picture hung above the couch to the pots in the kitchen. How had Sawyer not noticed this before?

He walked over to one of the large casement windows and pulled back the drape to look out on the busy street below. Streams of people walking this way and that, all of them in a hurry. Tomorrow he would go down and talk to Marian and Saint about coming back to work. It was time to rejoin the world. His mandatory leave was drawing to a close.

# Chapter Twelve

"Yeah, that's him," he confirmed.

"When did you take the picture?" the client asked.

"Last night. He opened up the drapes."

"What floor?"

"Third."

"Does he come out of the building at all?"

"Not since moving in."

"Well, we'll have to give him a reason to come out. Keep an eye on him. I'm sending an associate to take over from here."

"Associate for what, sir?"

"Nothing that involves you. Show him the building and the window where you saw Sawyer, and then your job is done. The remainder of your retainer will be deposited."

With a click, the call ended.

What the hell had he gotten himself into?

*** 

Today had been Sawyer's first day back to work, and any worries he had about how Alexander would treat him in front of everyone else were long gone. The big goof visited a few times, bringing him little plates of things off the menu for him to try.

He held nothing back, being affectionate in a way no one could miss, and told everyone Sawyer was his trusted taste tester. Sawyer could see how other kitchen staff would be terrified of telling the executive chef the bouillabaisse tasted like dirty socks.

Alexander's sister, Jillian, was back in town visiting. Sawyer was waiting for his chef to pick him up. She wanted to meet him, and tonight they were having a little get together at Alexander's condo before he took his sister to the airport to catch the last red-eye home.

Janice and Bobby had their whole evening planned. Sawyer's mind was at ease, knowing his brother was in good hands.

He'd thought about the risk of going over to Alexander's and discussed it with Bobby, Janice, and Marian, all of whom agreed that it should be safe considering he wouldn't be outside for long. Besides, it would give him a break from obsessing over the visits from the insurance company and Bobby's caseworker tomorrow.

Once he had those two squared away, Sawyer would begin their return to the real world and their one-bedroom apartment. Would Alexander want to visit him there? It wasn't exactly the best neighborhood.

It was mainly apartment buildings and a few corner stores, nothing fancy or new. Hard-working families mixed with the usual street element in DTLA. In some ways it'd become better, and in others it'd gotten worse over the past three years, but good people still lived there. The Garnet's were a prime example, even though their children had been trying to convince them to move down to Florida to be nearer to them.

Sawyer stood in the restaurant kitchen, waiting for Alexander to bring his car around back from the parking garage across the street. Detective Ross and Sam, Joey's boyfriend, and a third man walked by the kitchen doors as he stood there. It didn't seem strange until the three came back a couple of minutes later and approached him.

"Hey, Sawyer," Sam said. "You remember Detective Ross."

"I do," Sawyer said. "Good evening, Detective."

"Sawyer," Ross said. "I'd like to introduce you to a friend of mine, Detective Anders Nilsen. He's visiting from New York until after the holidays."

"Hi, Detective Nilsen," Sawyer greeted.

"Hey guys, what did I miss?" Alexander asked as he emerged from the back hallway to collect Sawyer.

"We were introducing Sawyer to a friend of mine from New York. He's going to be staying in one of the hub's spare rooms," Ross explained.

The tall man of obvious Scandinavian heritage held out his hand to Alexander. "Detective Anders Nilsen. Good to meet you."

Alexander shook his hand, and Sawyer did the same. "So, what brings you to the West Coast?"

"Had a couple of weeks of leave time to use up, and Ross had invited me to come out last year. Took a while, but I got here," Ander's said.

"That's great." Alexander looked at his watch. "Unfortunately, we have to go. My sister is waiting for us."

"No problem. We wanted to introduce Anders to both of you, so when you see him wandering around, you know who he is and that he's supposed to be here," Sam explained.

That made sense. If the guy was staying in the hub, Sawyer would've bumped into him eventually, and given what'd been going on, he would've freaked at seeing someone he didn't know.

Alexander led Sawyer through the back storerooms and to the reinforced door. The chef placed his hand on the palm scanner and waited for the bolts' click.

"You excited to meet Jillian?" he asked.

"Excited and nervous. You know." *Terrified.*

"It'll be fine. She's looking forward to meeting you. I told her all about you."

"Huh. Um, great." He felt nauseous.

"Cheer up. You'll see you're worrying for nothing," Alexander assured.

"I'll have to take your word for that."

Alexander wrapped his arm around Sawyer and led him down the back steps and to his car. Sawyer sucked in a deep breath of nearly fresh air—the Dumpsters were back here—and almost moaned. He'd been shut inside for too long. He was used to be out almost every day to go to work or do things with Bobby. Until now, he hadn't realized how much he missed it.

"Happy to be out again?" Alexander asked with a smile.

"Yeah." Sawyer could feel his spirits lifting.

"I'm sorry you have to be inside so much."

"You are the last person who needs to be sorry about anything," Sawyer said. "It won't always be this way."

"I love the way you try to find the bright side," Alexander responded before lowering his head and taking Sawyer's lips in a soft kiss. "Let's get you to my sister before she has a fit."

Alexander opened the passenger door of his black Audi A3, and Sawyer navigated easily into the spacious front seat. Sawyer was buckling his seat belt when he noticed a flash of light coming from the parking garage's second story. When Alexander opened the driver's door, Sawyer intended to tell him about it, but nothing was there when he looked back to check. Instead of seeming like a paranoid nutjob, he chalked it up to his mind playing tricks on him due to stress.

He wasn't going to ruin this night. He had a sister to impress.

"Ready?" Alexander asked, his smile genuine and happy.

"I am," Sawyer answered.

***

Alexander watched Sawyer's face as much as he dared without getting them into an accident. He worried about his boyfriend's reaction to the neighborhood. It screamed money. His sister had picked out the condo for him. He wasn't sure how to reassure Sawyer. Money mattered. No doubt about it. Those who had it always said it didn't. Clearly, their prism skewed differently than people who lived paycheck to paycheck. There wasn't a way to make Sawyer feel comfortable about the Larsen fortune, and Alexander wouldn't even try. He'd have to continue working on building their connection to show Sawyer people from different backgrounds had many things in common. Enough to adjust to the things that made them dissimilar.

He turned onto Wilshire Boulevard and passed the fairways of Los Angeles Country Club. In this area of Wilshire, tall buildings reached for the sky, and valets parked your car in your numbered spot in the garage below the building. Alexander slowed as he neared Thayer Avenue, and pulled into Ten Five-Sixty Wilshire, and drove up to the door where the valet was waiting.

Sawyer's gaze darted around nervously. Alexander asked, "Everything okay?"

Sawyer turned to look at him. "Sure. I've never been to this part of Wilshire before."

"It's a leased condo Jillian picked out. She liked the security and staff. I wasn't sure about the position at The Gates. I didn't want to invest in property. But now that I know it's a pain in the ass to get to The Gates from here," he shook his head, "I'm always stuck in traffic, which means I have to leave earlier and get home later... I wouldn't've signed the lease."

"I couldn't even imagine what a place like this goes for," Sawyer admitted.

"I'd be happy in a Craftsman," Alexander said. "I'm not all butlers and shit."

Sawyer leaned over and cupped the side of Alexander's face. "I know that."

The valet came over and opened Sawyer's door, and Alexander was quick to jump out and meet him on the other side. Taking his hand, Alexander led Sawyer into the building.

"Good evening, Mr. Larsen," John, his doorman, greeted them as they walked in. "Will you need anything this evening?"

"No, we're good, but I'll need my car in a couple of hours to take Sawyer home and Jillian to the airport."

"Call down, and we'll have it ready for you, sir."

"Thanks. I'd like to introduce Sawyer Hudson. I hope you'll be seeing more of him."

Sawyer raised his hand out to John. "Nice to meet you."

John smiled wide. "Very good to meet you as well, sir." His doorman seemed surprised, especially considering Cooper's behavior.

"Sawyer is fine."

"Understood, Sawyer."

Alexander could feel his excitement growing as he led Sawyer to the bank of elevators. As soon as the doors closed, he wrapped his arms around Sawyer's shoulders and said. "Thank you."

"For what?"

"For being you."

"It's all I know how to be," Sawyer said before laying his head against Alexander's shoulder. "You sure about this. We still have time to cut and run."

The elevator dinged as it stopped on Alexander's floor. "There's no chance that Jillian isn't going to love you. Trust me."

Sawyer looked up at him with those mysterious dark brown eyes. "Okay. I will."

Alexander knew they weren't talking about his sister any longer. "Thank you." The elevator doors began to close again, but he shot out his hand and stopped them. "Let's go."

Sawyer took hold of his hand, and Alexander led them down the hall and to his condo door. He touched the fob to the door and opened it to a scene straight out of a zany comedy. Smoke was in the air, something was beeping, his condo smelled like burnt charcoal, and his sister was running around in her bra and underwear waving a dishtowel in the air.

Sawyer shook his head before leading the way inside. "This is one hell of a welcome to the family."

# Chapter Thirteen

Sawyer wanted to laugh, but he wasn't too sure how Alexander's sister would take it. This scene had been on repeat for a while after he and his brother first started out alone. Sawyer couldn't cook, or at least he wasn't able to in his previous life. He'd improved over the years.

One look at the kitchen explained everything. Pots and pans covered the stove as they bubbled over, and ingredients were strewn all over the counter. The burned-out carcass of what Sawyer assumed had been a chicken was stuffed into the garbage pail sitting beside the stove.

Sawyer turned his head back around when he heard a scream.

"What the hell are you guys doing back here so soon?" Jillian asked as she tried to use the dishtowel to cover herself.

"It's seven, sis," Alexander said.

"Oh." She looked at Sawyer with disheveled hair and scanty attire and waved. "Hello, I'm Jillian. It's nice to meet you."

That's all it took. Sawyer couldn't hold back any longer and began laughing hard as he waved back and sputtered, "H..he...he...hello."

Soon Jillian joined in, and finally, Alexander broke out of his shock and began laughing too. Sawyer's worry floated away as their laughter grew, until all three were left gasping for air, and not due to the smoke which was fading fast—all the windows were open.

"So, what's for dinner?" Alexander asked while wiping the tears from his eyes.

"Pizza," Jillian deadpanned. "I think I'll go and put on some clothes."

"Good idea," Alexander said as he covered his eyes. "I don't want to watch my sister running around half-naked in front of my boyfriend."

"Don't drag me into this," Sawyer huffed.

"I'll be right back," Jillian said before running out of the room.

Sawyer turned to Alexander and asked, "I thought you said she liked to cook?"

"I did. Didn't say she was any good at it." Alexander chuckled and reached for the dishtowel Jillian had dropped. "I'll start in the kitchen.

"I'll order pizza," Sawyer said. "Got a favorite place? And what don't you or your sister like on yours?"

"No anchovies or fruit."

"You sure? It's going to suck without tomatoes," Sawyer teased as he pulled out his trusty flip phone.

"You know what I mean, like pineapples or pears," Alexander laughed. "And, no. No place in particular. Wait. Get over here. Something is moving on the floor, and I need your help identifying it."

"Shut up, asshole," Jillian yelled from down the hallway. "I'm not that bad."

Sawyer couldn't help the feeling happy standing in the middle of a disaster and chaos. They behaved the same as he and Bobby did, which went a long way to calm his nerves. Maybe this night had half a chance.

An hour and a half later, all three sat drinking coffee in the dining room, listening to Jillian recount adventures she and Alexander used to get into when they were younger. Her bags were packed and sitting by the front door.

"You took your dad's car when you were eight?" Sawyer asked.

"I stayed on the property," Alexander defended.

"A lot of good that did for the grass, gardens, and potted plants after you were done with your little joyride." Jillian waved her finger at her brother while maintaining a smile.

Sawyer liked how they teased each other. He could tell they'd grown up close. His perception of the Larsens was changing, and he realized that he'd been painting all rich people with the same brush.

"So, Sawyer," Jillian began, "what plans do you have for my brother?"

"Jillian," Alexander warned. "No interrogation."

Sawyer didn't take offense at her question. Jillian was Alexander's sister. She loved him and wanted the best for him, the same as Sawyer wanted for Bobby.

"I don't mind answering," Sawyer said while leaning forward. "My only plan is protecting my brother and caring for him. I wasn't looking for someone like your brother. Hell, I told him to stay away from me. I dated before the accident and have had zero dates since. Alexander wormed his way into my life. I can't tell you where we'll be in six days, let alone six months. We're making it up as we go along. The only thing I can assure you is I have no intention of using him or hurting him."

Jillian looked at him shrewdly. "Is my brother your priority?"

"He's a priority, but the person at the top of that list is, and will always be, my brother." Sawyer had been straight with Alexander from the start and saw no reason to treat his sister differently.

After a couple of moments of silence, Jillian cracked a smile. "Sibling bonds are forever, aren't they?"

"Yeah, they are."

"I like you. I respect how you've dealt with all that's been thrown at you. You're a strong man, and by all accounts, your brother is thriving. That's all because of you and your love for him. If my brother manages to keep you and earn a quarter of that love, he'd be a lucky man."

Sawyer was dumbfounded. He didn't know what to say. Thank you didn't seem to be enough, but it was all he had. "Ah, thanks."

Alexander reached overo and held Sawyer's hand. "I'm working on it."

"Good. Now it's time for me to go," Jillian said while picking her phone up from the couch cushion beside her.

"Okay, give me a second to have the car brought around," Alexander told her as he stood.

"No need. I have it all worked out," she said, and before Alexander could respond, there was a knock on the door. "That'll be John."

"I thought I was driving you?" Alexander went to answer the door.

"Last minute change of plans. I'm having a car service pick me up. Why don't you two take a bit of free time for yourselves?" Jillian grinned, much like her brother.

She slid into her coat as John collected her bags. "You two take care of each other. I'll be back for Christmas since you both will be working over the holidays, I presume."

Sawyer nodded because he'd be working every shift Marian gave him and was certain a few of those days would fall over the holiday.

"We have parties scheduled up to the twenty-fourth," Alexander said.

Jillian turned and wrapped her arms around Sawyer and whispered, "Take care of him for me."

"I will," Sawyer replied while hugging her back.

After another hug and kiss for Alexander, Jillian flew out the door in a flourish, followed by a smiling John. Alexander shut the door and took a minute before turning around.

Alexander looked worried. "You've got to believe me, Sawyer, I didn't plan this."

Ah. "I don't think that. Anyone who has ever met your sister would know better. She would have hauled your ass out of here if she picked up on anything about me she didn't like. She's your seal of approval."

Alexander let out a deep breath and walked over to him. "You know she's right. I would be lucky."

"So would I," Sawyer said without hesitation. Any concerns he had about allowing Alexander into his life...their lives, were distant memories.

Sawyer pulled his chef closer for a kiss that quickly turned heated. His hands roamed over Alexander's broad chest and shoulders. The man was perfect inside and out, and for the life of him, Sawyer couldn't remember why he'd been fighting this.

Alexander groaned as Sawyer worked his way across the chef's jaw and down his neck. Running his tongue over Alexander's warm salty skin and stopping to nibble here and there felt and tasted fantastic. He was out of practice, but his body was catching up.

As he reached Alexander's Adam's-apple Sawyer's phone chimed. He was certain the universe was fucking with him. Every time they locked lips, something came up, and it wasn't only his cock.

They slowed the kiss and eventually pulled apart. Sawyer reached into his pocket and pulled out his phone. A few clicks later and he was reading a text from Bobby.

"Everything okay?" Alexander asked.

"Yeah. This is from Janice's phone. Bobby's saying goodnight and suggested we stay out and have fun. He and Janice have called it a night and said they'd see us tomorrow."

"Could my sister be working with those two?"

"I don't think so," Sawyer said, tearing his gaze away from the screen and looked back into those blue beauties. "What do you want to do?"

Alexander grinned. Apparently, he had a few ideas. "Do you want to watch a movie and relax?"

Nice. No pressure. Take it slow. Show you care. Much appreciated. But... Sawyer had other things in mind that had nothing to do with a television. The only problem: Sawyer was rusty in the romance department. They were both adults. Why did this have to be so difficult?

"Sure, maybe you can show me your *Star Wars* and superhero collections."

Without the distraction of the burnt chicken and Jillian running around in her underwear, Sawyer took in the condo's décor and noticed glass cases against one wall in the spacious living room. The furniture was comfortable and homey, not polished and perfect, which he loved. The more he got to know Alexander, the less he fit into the mold of how Sawyer believed people with money behaved. Or at least in his and Jillian's case.

The dark hardwood floors were covered in cozy area rugs, and the tall drapes were open, giving him a peek at the large, rounded balcony.

"Right this way," Alexander smiled wide and led him over to the cases.

The first thing that drew his attention was the full-sized Darth Vader helmet, and along its side was the signature of Dave Prowse, Darth Vader himself.

"Now that's cool," Sawyer said before moving on to what looked like a Blaster Gun, complete with another signature. "Who signed that?"

"Harrison Ford."

There were miniature TIE fighters, Millennium Falcon, Death Star, R2-D2, C-3PO, Chewbacca, lightsabers, action figures still in their original boxes, and on and on. Alexander's collection was extensive, and if his brother were here, he'd be on cloud nine.

"Wow, Bobby would love to see this," Sawyer said. "Is that a signed copy of the *Star Wars: A New Hope* script?"

"Yes," Alexander answered. "The first time I saw *Star Wars*, I was hooked. My dream of traveling to distant planets and meeting all these strange people constituted my dream life for a long time. Maybe we could bring Bobby over here sometime so that he can see it for himself. What do you think?"

"I think he'll never want to leave," Sawyer joked as he neared a second cabinet.

A life-sized Captain America shield sat at the center of this collection, an Infinity Gauntlet lay on the shelf to the right, and a Mjolnir, Thor's hammer, was to the left. Several superhero figures were intermixed with signed comic books and pictures of the original five Avengers: Iron Man, Ant-Man, the Wasp, Hulk, and Thor.

"As you can see, I'm the biggest geek." Alexander smiled but looked uncertain of Sawyer's reaction.

Was he worried this would be a turn-off? Sawyer didn't want Alexander to worry about showing his passions. Like cooking, it appeared he put a focused effort into curating this collection.

"Not even close," Sawyer said. "I'll let you in on a little secret. I like geeks."

"You do," the big man laughed, moving closer. "Will I get bonus points if I tell you I have a life-sized R-two D-two, and C-three P0 stored back at my parents' house?"

"It couldn't hurt," Sawyer teased.

Alexander smiled, and with a few quick moves and Sawyer found himself in Alexander's arms, pressed against his hard body.

"You make me happy," Alexander said before taking Sawyer's lips in a deep, wet kiss that left him a bit unstable on his feet. "Ready for a movie?"

"Okay," Sawyer agreed. "But anytime you feel the need to show me how happy you are, you go right ahead."

Alexander's laugh was loud, filling the room and warming Sawyer's heart. Damn, this man could become a serious addiction.

"Here," Alexander said while pulling a drawer open from underneath his wall unit. "I'll get us a few drinks. I bought the beer I saw you drinking the other day at your condo. Would you like one?"

Sawyer stopped his perusal of DVDs to look at Alexander. "You made sure to have my beer here for me. Are you for real? No one would have ever thought of that."

With his grin in place, Alexander said, "My pleasure."

# Chapter Fourteen

Alexander took a sip of scotch and settled back onto the couch with the man who had become an important part of his life. Of course, logically, their relationship was moving faster than fast, but as Charles Darwin once wrote, "A man who dares to waste one moment of time has not discovered the value of life."

Sawyer had chosen the original Spider-Man trilogy starring Tobey Maguire for them to watch. Alexander was enjoying sitting with his arm around his boyfriend and relaxing after a busy day. He'd like to do more of this in the future.

It had been hard controlling his desire, but until Sawyer gave him the go-ahead, there would be nothing more than cuddling. He respected that it'd been a long time since Sawyer had been with anyone, and Alexander would never pressure him. He was lucky to be here doing this, particularly considering their rocky start.

As they watched Tobey swing from buildings around New York City, Sawyer's hand began wandering. He laid the palm of his hand on Alexander's knee, and moments later, Sawyer's index finger began tracing figure eights up his thigh. Alexander didn't have a hope in hell of keeping his hard-on under wraps.

"Any higher, and I can't promise I won't lay you down on this couch."

"Maybe that's the point," Sawyer replied.

That response sent a sizzle of heat firing through his veins, but Alexander had to make sure they were on the same page. "I'm going to need you to spell it out for me."

Sawyer looked up with those dark brown eyes that reminded Alexander of fine chocolate and said, "I want you. Preferably in the bedroom where we have more room to explore."

"I want you, too. I want to make love to you until we both pass out." Alexander wanted to give Sawyer a night of passion, and then many more nights after that. He reached over and took Sawyer's beer out of his hand and set it down on the coffee table.

Sawyer turned to press his chest against Alexander's side before kissing his way up Alexander's neck. "I could get behind those plans."

That was all the confirmation Alexander needed as he leaned down to take Sawyer's soft lips in a kiss showing him how much Alexander wanted him. By the hard cock pressing against his leg, it appeared Sawyer indeed wanted him too.

"Let's go to the bedroom," Alexander said. This couldn't be comfortable with his brace.

"Lead the way." Sawyer wasn't holding back, and Alexander loved it.

He stood, held out his hand, and pulled Sawyer up from the couch and into his waiting arms. He couldn't help but dive in for another kiss. Sawyer's red, swollen lips begged for his attention.

When they broke apart, Alexander had enough sense to continue to lead Sawyer to his newly furnished bedroom. He didn't bother turning on the lights. They were on the fifteenth floor, the moon was full, and the hazy light flooded in from the streets below and around them, creating an almost ethereal glow.

Alexander sat Sawyer down on the end of the bed. He then went to his knees in front of him before capturing his luscious mouth once again. When they broke apart, both were gasping for air. It was too soon to be contemplating love, but here it was slapping him in the face.

"If you undo your jeans, we can slide them down, and I can help you remove your brace," he suggested.

Sawyer didn't hesitate. He undid the button and lowered the zipper. Alexander had him lie back on the bed while he navigated the jeans past Sawyer's hips, over the brace, and down his legs. Once he'd removed his jeans, Alexander got his first look at Sawyer's new brace on him and the multitude of scars crisscrossing his leg underneath.

"Doesn't look too sexy, does it?" Sawyer asked, his tone unsure.

No way would Alexander allow the man he was quickly falling in love with feel less in any way. "Your leg doesn't define whether you're sexy or not. You're the whole package. Don't sell yourself short." Alexander kissed Sawyer's knee before helping him remove the brace, and then finally, he had Sawyer scooch up to the top of the bed.

"Take your shirt off, baby," Alexander asked, and Sawyer happily complied.

"Now it's your turn," Sawyer ordered, his voice deeper than usual.

"Anything you want," Alexander said and began shedding his clothing right down to his boxer-briefs.

Sawyer's eyes were drinking him in as he stepped to the end of the bed and began crawling up and over him. There were four long scars at Sawyer's ankle that ran up to his calf. Alexander started there. Slowly he licked and kissed his way up Sawyer's leg, and by the moans and breathy huffs, he was enjoying this as much as Alexander was.

Alexander wanted to show Sawyer that his leg wasn't ugly or anything to be ashamed of around him or anyone. "You're stunning, every inch of you." Alexander looked up to find his lover watching him closely. "Every inch of you, Sawyer."

He carried on with his plan to kiss every scar on Sawyer's leg, from his ankle to his hip. When Alexander made it to his lover's waist, the evidence of Sawyer's need was barely contained by his underwear.

"That's it, baby," Alexander moaned as he palmed Sawyer's hard-on. "I'll take care of this for you."

Alexander leaned over Sawyer's body and took in his handsome face. "I need you."

"Show me what you got," Sawyer whispered before pushing up for a kiss Alexander was more than willing to give.

He reached over to the side table and pulled out a new bottle of lube and a condom, and set them both by Sawyer's hip. Alexander then slipped off his underwear, allowing his throbbing cock freedom before doing the same with Sawyer's, causing the sexy man to hiss when his cock slapped against his abdomen.

Without waiting another moment, Alexander took Sawyer's beautiful cock down his throat. Sawyer's back bowed off the bed, and Alexander placed his hand on Sawyer's stomach to keep him in place.

Alexander used his tongue to explore the mushroomed head of Sawyer's cock dipping his tongue into the slit at the top and then sucking him down to the base. He reached for the lube, squeezed out a fair amount considering Sawyer's comment about not dating since the accident, and set about sending his lover to the moon.

Timing his fingers' advance with deep, strong pulls of Sawyer's cock helped distract the man from any possible discomfort, and slowly Sawyer opened to him. Once one finger slid in freely, he added another until Sawyer's hands were clutching at the sheets, and his head was thrown back moaning in ecstasy.

Once Alexander found his lover's gland, he pegged it ruthlessly until Sawyer began crying out for him to bury his cock deep in him while simultaneously throwing the condom at Alexander. That's exactly where he wanted Sawyer, lost in need from all the pleasure he was receiving.

Alexander stuffed a thick pillow underneath Sawyer's hips, hoping to ease any pressure on his leg. Then, after rolling the condom down his cock, Alexander lined himself up with Sawyer's hole and asked. "Ready, baby?"

Sawyer looked at him with unfocused eyes, his face flushed and lips swollen, and said, "I want you in every way possible."

Alexander's heart skipped a beat as he leaned down and began kissing Sawyer as he slowly slid himself inside his lover. Sawyer's breaths turned into pants, and when Alexander bottomed out, his moans of pleasure joined the chorus.

Raising his head, Alexander looked down at Sawyer. "You okay?"

Sawyer's smile said it all. "I will be when you start moving."

Alexander chuckled. "Yes, sir."

Slowly, he pulled out, watching for any signs that Sawyer might be in pain. When he saw none, Alexander pushed back inside, making Sawyer's eyes roll back in his head as his moans increased in both volume and intensity.

Soon they had a rhythm, and as they sped up, Alexander was sure to lift Sawyer's leg and brace it in his arm as not to jar it. He shifted his hips until he found Sawyer's sweet spot once again, making the man holler.

"I'm going to come," Sawyer cried out.

Alexander wrapped his free hand around Sawyer's cock and pumped in time with his thrusts. "That's it, baby, come for me."

Sawyer's cock pulsed in Alexander's hand at the same time his ass squeezed Alexander's cock tight until he was almost unable to move. Each stream of come that flowed from the tip of Sawyer's cock drove him higher until Alexander's balls began throbbing, sending a rush of electricity up his spine, through his body, and out his cock as he came buried deep inside of Sawyer.

Alexander released Sawyer's cock so he could lean on that arm above Sawyer. He wasn't quite ready to disconnect from his lover. Sawyer's eyes were closed, but the smile still glued to his face, assured Alexander his man was feeling good.

Once he got his breathing under control, Alexander gently lowered Sawyer's leg to the mattress and pulled out. He dealt with the condom and crawled up to lie beside a sleepy Sawyer.

Pulling the blanket over them, Alexander opened his arms when Sawyer rolled over to lay his head on Alexander's chest. A contented sigh followed by Sawyer's arms pulling him closer made his heart fly.

"How's your leg?" It would gut him if he'd hurt Sawyer.

"A bit tender."

"Shit, I'm sorry." He should've been more careful.

Sawyer raised his head and looked at him. "There's nothing to be sorry over. You make me feel like a whole man again. We'll have to experiment with different positions until we find what works, but that's part of the fun."

"Experiment, huh? Well, I'm the man for the job."

"I thought you might be," Sawyer's said as he wiggled his eyebrows. "Now, whatcha going to do with it?"

"I'd be more than happy to show you," Alexander growled playfully as he rolled Sawyer onto his back and plundered his lips.

This was going to be a night of the best research he'd ever been asked to do.

\*\*\*

The next morning Sawyer and Alexander made it back to The Gates before Ms. Winters arrived at nine. Sawyer would be lying if he said he wasn't freaking out. A representative from the insurance company and Rachel from Family Services would be here in a little over two hours.

Sawyer hoped it wasn't the same guy they usually sent out. Richard Casey. He liked to toy with Sawyer whenever he'd asked for something Bobby needed. "We'll have to wait and see," or "I doubt that's covered, so don't get your hopes up," to "Give me a reason to want to put this receipt through for you." Whatever his problem, the jerk got his jollies off the power he held.

After a quick shower and change of clothes, Sawyer felt more like himself. Alexander had dressed in a suit and cut quite the imposing figure when he wanted to. Sawyer and Bobby wore their best clothes, which wasn't anywhere near as fancy, but they cleaned up well.

Janice had left ten minutes ago for a much-needed day off. Although she never complained, Sawyer knew how stressful this whole situation was for everyone.

Sawyer walked around the condo to make sure everything was spotless. "Maybe I should dust again."

"You don't need to do anything," Alexander said from the dining room table. "The condo doesn't look lived in already."

"Oh god, should I put some stuff out, so they don't think this is some sort of fake living arrangement?" He knew he was obsessing but was powerless to stop himself.

Alexander stood and walked over to stand in front of him. "I was joking, Sawyer. Everything looks perfect. Try to relax a bit before Ms. Winters gets here."

"I've never had a lawyer before. Sure, there was my parents' estate after they died, but nothing like this. She's coming here to advocate for us, not simply doling out what a piece of paper says."

"You'll never have to face anything alone again," Alexander assured while cupping Sawyer's jaw. "I promise."

A knock on the door almost made Sawyer jump. He was wound tight and edgy. What would the insurance representative threaten him with today? Since Sawyer was the one who punched Cooper in front of the media, it could be anything.

Alexander went over and answered the door, and moments later, a woman with a grandma vibe stepped into the condo. She wasn't particularly tall or imposing to look at, and he felt his stomach drop.

"Sawyer, I'd like to introduce Ms. Ruth Winters," Alexander began. "She will be your counsel from this point forward."

Sawyer stuck out his hand, and she took it in a light grip."

"It's so nice to finally meet you. Don't worry. Today's the day of reckoning for a few people." Her eyes twinkled, which matched the shine of her white-blonde hair.

"Why don't you set up over on the dining room table, Ruth," Alexander suggested before leading her over.

Once she began unpacking her rolling briefcase, Alexander returned with a knowing smile on his face.

"I thought you said Ms. Winters was ruthless, not that her name was Ruth, and she looks like she bakes cookies for children in her spare time." He was going to have an anxiety attack any second.

Alexander laughed before saying, "Trust me to have your back and your best interests in mind when choosing someone from our legal team to represent you and Bobby."

Speaking of Bobby, he came racing down the hallway, his wheelchair's motor working whirring. "Is our lawyer here? Is she ready to kick butt?"

Ruth laughed and said, "You bet I am." She walked over and shook hands with his brother.

"I wanna see that insurance guy squirm for once instead of us," Bobby stated, obviously not sharing the concerns Sawyer had.

"I can guarantee there will be copious amounts of squirming. You might even catch a stray tear if we're lucky," Ruth said. Of course, that's what Sawyer wanted to hear, but he'd prefer to hear it from a six-foot-tall warrior in armor.

"I call front row for this show," Bobby said as he followed Ruth back to the dining room. "Can I help?"

"Trust me?" Alexander asked.

Sawyer sucked in a deep breath and let it out slowly. "I do."

Alexander winked at him. "Remember that on our wedding day."

"You're insane," Sawyer huffed. "We've only been dating for like a week."

"The best week of my life," Alexander said without a hint of sarcasm.

Sawyer wrapped his arms around Alexander. "It's been memorable, that's for sure."

"Come on, let's go see what Ruth has dug up," Alexander said, taking Sawyer's hand.

Dug up seemed to be the best way to describe this situation, considering Mr. Richard Casey had buried them under a truckload of paperwork. Most of which he didn't understand.

Sawyer half expected Ruth to pull out knitting needles to work on a Christmas sweater.

# Chapter Fifteen

Alexander watched the expressions on Sawyer's and Bobby's faces as Ruth laid out what she'd found on the table in front of them. Shocked and confused was an understatement. It was ten-thirty in the morning, giving them precious little time before their visitors came knocking. Miguel had said he'd keep an eye out for them and bring them up when they arrived as he'd done for Ruth.

"Are you okay," Alexander asked them when neither had spoken.

Sawyer turned to look at him from across the table. He opened his mouth to say something, but their cellphones began ringing. Alexander read the message on his phone's screen. Shit.

"They're here already," Sawyer growled, his hand shaking as it held onto his phone.

"They're early," Bobby said.

"I imagine in order to catch you two off guard," Ruth said with a grin. "Won't they be surprised to find us all here waiting for them?"

"Is it that Richard guy," Bobby asked, and Alexander didn't miss the anger in the teenager's voice.

"Yep, that's the business card he gave to Miguel," Sawyer said as he looked down at his phone. "You're right, Ruth, his day of reckoning has come."

Sawyer and Ruth shared a devious smile.

"Stick to the plan," Ruth said as she pulled her knitting from her bag. "I want to see how far he intends to go."

"I knew you had knitting needles in that bag," Sawyer declared, making Ruth laugh.

"I never go anywhere without them," she said. "You'd be surprised what you hear when society views you as old and weak."

"I'm sorry, Ruth," Sawyer mumbled, "for ever doubting you."

This time when the knock came, they were ready. Today would be the day the Hudson brothers finally got justice.

*\*\*\**

Sawyer calmly walked to the door and answered it, knowing full well who'd be waiting for him. The anger bubbling inside of him was barely contained, but he wanted to see this through. He pushed down his roiling emotions and plastered a smile on his face.

He reached for the handle and opened the door, and saw Miguel. Behind him, Richard Casey and Rachel, Bobby's caseworker.

"Are you ready for visitors, Sawyer?" Miguel asked. "If not, I'll be happy to take these two back downstairs."

Sawyer could hear Richard's huff, which only made Miguel smile wider. Sawyer couldn't help but smile back and soak in the camaraderie the Marine was sharing with him.

"Thank you for all of this, Miguel," Sawyer said, meaning more than this one thing. "They can come in."

Miguel nodded and stepped back out of the way. Sawyer could have sworn he heard the big guy growl when Richard Casey went by him. These people here at The Gates took backing your play to a whole new level.

"Excuse me," Richard said. "Did you growl at me?"

Miguel looked at Richard as if he were insane.

"I didn't hear anything," Sawyer said. "Are you feeling all right, Mr. Casey?"

"I'm fine," he hissed. "All of this is irregular, Sawyer. This building is a highly unusual environment for Bobby to be living in." There was nothing odd about condos above restaurants in LA.

"I find it charming," Rachel said as she walked in. "These old stone buildings are stunning, and it's nice to see it's getting a new lease on life."

Sawyer had always thought Rachel was a nice person, but he couldn't separate her from Richard. They were both trying to take Bobby away from him.

"We're set up in the dining room," Sawyer said. "Please follow me."

"We?" Richard asked.

"Yes, Bobby, my boyfriend, and my legal counsel."

"Legal counsel," Richard hummed. "I guess it's time to play hardball, Sawyer. I've protected you long enough."

Sawyer knew the guy was trying to threaten and scare him, so he played along. "She's an old friend of my parents who's in town." *Nothing threatening at all, Richard.*

When they approached the table, Alexander stood while Ruth continued to knit. All signs of their paperwork and files were gone. In their place, bottles of water and a bundt cake. Where the hell did they get a bundt cake? The entire scene made everything appear more like a social gathering than a serious meeting.

"Hello, Bobby," Rachel said. "It's so nice to see you again. Do you mind if we go to your room and have a talk about all these big changes you've had?"

This was the typical way of their meetings. While Richard talked to Sawyer, Rachel took Bobby away to have a private chat. According to Bobby, she mainly wanted to know how he was feeling most of the time, and his health."

"Sure, Rachel. My new bedroom is down this way," Bobby agreed while backing his wheelchair away from the dining table and leading her down the hall.

"So, where to begin, Sawyer," Richard said as he eyed Alexander and Ruth. "I don't believe we need your boyfriend here for this meeting." The fucker used air quotes when he said, boyfriend. "Both professionally and personally, I don't condone such behavior.

"I want him to stay," Sawyer said. "I believe that is my right." Let's play, asshole.

"I'm staying," Alexander stated, flat out. Neither his voice nor his expression left room for discussion.

Richard took a second look at Ruth, who appeared oblivious. "Is he part of your legal team?"

"No, I'm a chef downstairs," Alexander answered.

Richard's usual indifference quickly covered up his look of relief. "Fine, he can stay for now. Let's get down to it. You assaulted a man at the zoo. Do you deny it, Sawyer?"

"No." There was no chance of looking at it any other way.

Richard seemed shocked by how easy it was to get that confession out of him, but his smile became cruel. "You admit to physically assaulting a man at the zoo?"

"Yes," Sawyer repeated. "Do you want to know why?'

"I don't give a rat's ass why you did it, Sawyer. You put your brother in danger, and I warned you that your irresponsible ways would cause me to recommend Bobby be removed from your care."

Before Sawyer could say anything, Alexander cut in. "Sawyer has never been irresponsible. It's not in his nature."

"I don't care what his nature is," Richard hissed. "Bobby would be safer in an appropriate institution where he can be supervised. This has to do with Bobby's welfare, plain and simple. My hands are tied."

"How about handcuffed instead of tied, Mr. Casey?" Ruth said as she folded her knitting. "With Bobby out of the way, no one would ever suspect what you've done."

"What I've done?" Richard asked. "You sure this old friend isn't senile? Be careful how you speak to me because I can suggest to the courts supervised visits or perhaps none at all."

"It's so easy to sit back and judge people as useless if they have a disability or are over a certain age, Mr. Casey. You believe no one cares, so that leaves you free to do whatever you wish with them." Ruth carried on as if Richard hadn't even spoken. Sawyer loved her.

"Enough rambling from an old woman. I came here today to inform you that I will be going forward with my recommendation to remove Bobby from your custody, Sawyer, and to become a ward of the state."

It took everything inside of Sawyer to hold back, and he was busy squeezing the blood out of Alexander's hand to keep himself seated. Ruth leaned over and handed her bag to Alexander who pulled out a stack of papers and threw them on the table in front of Richard.

He picked them up and growled, "What the hell is this?"

Ruth sat up straight, and her demeanor changed in an instant. No longer the kindly grandmother knitting a sweater, Ruth was now on the hunt and deadly serious.

"You've been served, Mr. Richard Casey," she said while looking down at her beeping phone. "And that confirms that the parent company holding the Hudson brother's insurance policy has been as well."

"How long did you think you could get away with this," Sawyer growled. "You would have taken my brother away to hide your little secret."

"I don't know what you're talking about," Richard said calmly, but his body language screamed he wanted to run. Sawyer knew that look.

"You have been siphoning money away from Mr. Sawyer Hudson and Mr. Bobby Hudson's monthly entitlement. There's also a matter of a missing ninety-six thousand, five hundred and eighty-two dollars, and thirteen cents." Ms. Ruth Winters was kicking ass, and Sawyer could see what Alexander meant by trusting him.

"Tricking me into appointing you as our conservator," Sawyer said as he stood. "I'd like to see which judge pushed that through."

"Don't worry, we will soon enough," Ruth said. "There's always a trail left behind."

Ruth was a shark, and she'd tasted blood. She began throwing out the section numbers of his parents' life insurance policy that had been ignored or looted. Also, something called Forensic Accounting, which Sawyer had no clue about. Then she went on to how a jury would react to the fact that Richard had approached Sawyer even before he was out of the hospital. Then stolen from two disabled men who'd lost their parents. The more she talked, the whiter Richard became until he zoned in on Sawyer again.

"If it's the last thing I do, I'll make sure you never see your brother again." His eyes were squinted, and his lips a slash across his trembling face. "You've fucked with the wrong person."

"No, you won't," an angry voice said from behind them. "You won't hurt these brothers."

Sawyer turned to find Rachel and Bobby behind them in the hallway.

"Shut up. This doesn't involve you bleeding hearts over at DCHS," Richard yelled.

Rachel took a couple of steps forward. "You've been lying to me. Sending in reports about mishandled money on Sawyer's part and how he couldn't be trusted to have Bobby's best interest at heart. The accusations of neglect and addiction were lies. You used DCHS to keep the pressure on these people to hide what you've done. No one is going to separate these brothers. You have my word on that." Rachel was on their side. Thank God.

Mr. Casey looked ready to blow. His control was slipping. He got a crazy look in his eyes and lunged out of his chair straight at Sawyer. Alexander was up out of his chair and placing himself in front of Sawyer. After a weak attempt at taking on Alexander, Richard gave up when he'd been thrown to the floor.

"Call Miguel," Alexander ordered, and Sawyer pushed the last number on his cellphone.

"What's wrong?" Miguel's voice boomed over the speaker.

"We need you and the police."

"On my way."

Sawyer walked over to Bobby, leaned down and hugged him. "No one is ever going to take you from me. No one."

# Chapter Sixteen

It had been five days since the confrontation with Richard Casey, and the evil man was still sitting in jail. The insurance company worked quickly to distance themselves from their employee's actions and offered their complete cooperation into the ensuing investigation.

Bobby had seen justice served when Richard was arrested and taken away. Sawyer could tell the difference in his brother since the stress had been removed.

In the meantime, the holiday season was in full swing, and the restaurant was busy. Sawyer barely had time to taste Alexander's dishes when he brought them over. It felt like everyone was celebrating and having get-togethers at The Gates.

Who could blame them, though? The atmosphere was matched by the delicious food Alexander and his team created in the kitchen. It'd been another long night, and the place was still full of diners.

A scraping sound caught his attention, and Sawyer turned around to find Marian dragging four bags of garbage through the back on her way to the Dumpster outside.

"Hold on, and I'll give you a hand," Sawyer said while pushing another tray of plates into the dishwasher.

Marian stopped and waited for him. "Thank you. I hate disturbing you like this, but I can't seem to find anyone else who's available."

"No problem, ma'am. I don't mind helping you at all," Sawyer said as he came over and took three of the four bags. "Lead the way."

She grabbed hold of the fourth bag, led the way back through the storerooms, and scanned her palm to let them out the back door. The night was cool, and he felt the sweat on his shirt stick to his back. Carefully, he navigated his way down the back stairs to join Marian at the bottom.

"The temperature is dropping fast," Marian said. "I hate to think of all the street people out in this, and it's only going to get worse. Finn has a charity that delivers meals to the homeless on Skid Row. We were going to step up to two times a week over the holidays. Would you and Bobby like to help out?"

Sawyer had known about the wonderful things Finn had accomplished and would be proud to help. "Sure. We'd love to."

"Excellent, young man," she assured. "There's always a spot for everyone."

"Thank you for thinking of us," Sawyer said as they neared the Dumpsters.

He was throwing the third bag in when a car came speeding into the back lot. Sawyer went to stand in front of Marian, but the older woman reached down and pulled out her knife. Right, she could protect herself.

A tall, dark-haired man jumped out of the driver's side, holding a gun on them. "Mr. Hudson, get into the car."

"He isn't going anywhere," Marian hissed, the knife firmly in her right hand.

"I will kill the old woman if you refuse. Decide now," he said as he pointed the gun straight at Marian.

"No. Don't hurt her. I'll come with you."

Marian grabbed his arm when he went to walk by her. "You can't go."

"Please, take care of Bobby for me."

Sawyer removed her hand and walked over to the passenger door of the car, and got in. All the while, the stranger had his gun trained on Marian. When he shut the door, it locked, sealing him in there.

His kidnapper backed his way to the driver's side and got in, threw it into drive, and spun out of the lot.

"Someone wishes to speak with you, Mr. Hudson," the man said while holding the gun in his hand and pointing it at Sawyer's stomach. "You stay still, and we'll get along fine."

Who the hell else wanted to fuck with him? It wasn't as if he knew a lot of people. Years of solitude blown out the window in a matter of weeks. What the hell?

Sawyer was about to ask who the mystery person was when he felt a slight prick to the back of his neck. Instantly his vision blurred, and moments before he passed out, he heard his kidnapper laughing.

"Night, night."

\*\*\*

Sawyer was so cold. He reached for his blankets but came away with nothing but air. He cracked his sore eyes open, wondering if he was having another migraine because his head was pounding. When his vision cleared, he realized he was lying on a piece of cardboard on the floor of a dilapidated room. Tiles hung down from the ceiling, the skeletal metal holders having long since given up. The drywall was torn from the studs, and what looked to be long horizontal shelves hung by a single screw in its right upper corner.

Where the hell was he? Sawyer confirmed he was alone from the bit of light streaming in through the holes in the roof. His memories came flooding back in one horrifying moment, and he pushed himself up onto his feet. Thankfully, he still had his brace. Whatever was out there, he would face it on his feet. With a quick check to confirm the door was locked, he searched for options.

He allowed himself only a moment to worry about Bobby and Alexander before he got his head back into survival mode. He needed a weapon. There was nothing usable at first glance, but the boarded-up pass-through window gave him an idea. With all his strength and using his shoulder for leverage, Sawyer pushed up on the exposed piece of the windowsill. The piece of lumber groaned, making him worry about alerting whoever had him that he was awake, but he didn't stop until he came away with a two by four in his hands.

He felt a bit better now that he had something to fight with. Now to figure out how to get out of here. A scratching noise caught his attention, and it was coming from the far corner. When he drew closer, it turned into a buzzing, and for a moment, Sawyer thought there was a beehive in here until he saw the tip of the saw blade.

Why would someone be trying to break into the room? Then it hit him: he was being rescued.

"Hello," he whispered next to the wall.

"Stand back. I'm getting you out."

Sawyer didn't recognize the voice. Maybe it was the cops, but why wouldn't they come through the locked front door?

"Who are you, and where is the other guy?"

"I'm the one getting you out of there before the other guy gets back."

Sawyer wasn't about to argue with that. "Where are we?"

"Rock-a-Hoola Waterpark in Newberry Springs," he said, never once stopping the cutting. He'd already cut one side and now was on to the other.

"Newberry Springs, that's hours away from DTLA."

"Yeah, well, the tracker I put on big, tall, and scary's car had a bit of a glitz, so I'm a little late to the party," he said before turning off what Sawyer presumed was an electric skill saw. "Okay, watch out. I'm going to kick this in."

Sawyer got out of the way as his rescuer began kicking the cut wood piece in the wall. After a few good hits, the wood broke and fell into the room. When he ran to the door, Sawyer found a smaller man lying on his back with his feet up against the wood from where he'd kicked it free. He had long blond hair tied up in a ponytail and brilliant green eyes. This would have been his last guess as to who his rescuer was. There wasn't a thing about him that screamed ex-military or police as Sawyer had hoped.

"Perfect, lie down and give me your hands, and I'll pull you through the hole," the stranger suggested while reaching out with his hands.

He had to put his piece of lumber down, his only weapon. What if this was all a game put together by his kidnapper? What if the person who wanted to talk to him was out there waiting?

"Come on. We're running out of time."

Sawyer struggled to decide, and Bobby's words came back to him. *Sometimes you have to take a chance.*

"Okay," he yelled and threw away his weapon. "I'm coming out."

Sawyer lay down on the dust-covered floor and stuck his hands out the hole so he could be pulled free. Someone grabbed his hands and began pulling. It took the smaller guy a few tries to pull him out, but eventually, Sawyer was in the early morning pre-dawn. The sun hadn't risen yet, but the sky was no longer dark.

The stranger helped Sawyer to his feet. "Thank you."

"Let's get out of here," the man said.

"Wait, who are you?"

"My name is Trey Stoneham."

"The reporter?"

"Yep. Now let's go."

"Is this a trick?"

"No, I need us to start moving," Trey said as he peeked around the corner and ran to a building roughly twenty feet away before waving at him to follow.

The only way to find out what's going on was to get answers from the reporter/rescuer, so Sawyer followed. When he reached the second building, he looked back to see an old arcade sign out front of the building he'd been locked in.

There were a few buildings and what looked to be old concession stands scattered around. Exposed pipes and concrete hint to where the water slides might have been while cement pools lay dry and empty. There was even an old lazy river.

"Why are you helping me?" Sawyer asked. "Weren't you the one wanted to write the big expose on who I was?"

"Yep, in the beginning," Trey agreed. "I'm a reporter, and it's my job to find the answers."

"Don't you ever consider the lives you effect by that bullshit you wrote about a love triangle?"

"Yep, but unless I sell articles, I don't get paid. If I don't get paid, several other people are affected. Look, I didn't mean for any of this to happen. That's why I'm here to get you out."

Trey scanned the area before heading to what might have been the changing rooms and bathrooms. Sawyer followed when he waved him over. He couldn't match Trey's speed with his leg, but the guy waited for him.

"How are you involved in any of this?"

"In my spare time, I'm a private investigator, but that doesn't pay the bills. When I was approached to stake out The Gates for any sign of you, I thought it was a win-win considering you were already on my radar."

"You spied on me?"

"Yep, that's what we do."

"You're an asshole."

"I don't disagree."

That threw Sawyer off. He'd expected a fight, not a confirmation.

"You work for the guys who kidnapped me?"

"No. I took a PI contract to locate you. Once I did, I was out. That was the end of my involvement."

"Then what the hell are you doing here now?"

"Fixing a mistake," Trey said before running even further away from the front of the abandoned park.

Sawyer limped and followed him. They went past what might have been an old hotdog cart lying on its side and rusting into the ground. The place was covered in graffiti, so it must have visitors, but where were they?

"My car is up over that hill," Trey explained while pointing into the distance. "If we're separated, you head that way. The keys are on top of the front driver's wheel."

"There's no way I could beat you there."

That's when Sawyer heard the sound of a car driving in. "Shit, he's back."

Trey pulled a small gun out of his boot and looked at Sawyer. "You keep going. If I don't make it to the car by the time you reach it drive away to the nearest police station."

"But—."

"This isn't a second guess kind of situation, Sawyer. Here, take this," Trey said while holding out a knife. "Just in case."

Trey didn't wait for Sawyer to answer. Instead, he turned around and ran back in the opposite direction. Sawyer wasn't sure what to do. He was useless in a fight with his leg in a brace, but he couldn't let Trey face his kidnapper alone.

# Chapter Seventeen

Alexander watched as Detective Ross and Detective Anders Nilsen set up a command center in The Gates's office. Captain Eric Meyers and Officer Sam Webb were on their phones while Miguel and James stood at the ready. Cruisers were combing the streets for any sign of Sawyer or the vehicle Marian had described considering it didn't have plates when the kidnapper took Sawyer.

Time was slipping away, and Alexander was no closer to having his love back in his arms. He wasn't in the military or an officer, so his abilities were limited, but Alexander intended to be right there when they got Sawyer back.

Alexander's phone began ringing, and he pulled it out of his pocket to answer it. "Hello."

"He's gone," Jillian's voice came over the speaker he'd accidentally hit.

"Who's gone?"

"Cooper Hitchford," she replied, getting everyone's attention.

"Sis, you're on speaker. Sawyer has been kidnapped, and the police are here trying to find him."

"It has to be Cooper. His family hasn't seen him in two days, and his condo is empty."

"I need more information on this Cooper Hitchford and why he would like to harm Sawyer," Captain Meyers stated.

"Okay, sis, I have to let you go. I'll call if anything changes."

"Okay, love you, bro."

"Love you."

When Alexander looked up, Miguel was already recounting the sordid details bringing everyone up to speed. Bobby and Janice were upstairs in the condo, waiting on word. They'd had to call in Bobby's doctor to calm him before he made himself sicker.

It seemed like everyone was on the phone, sending out orders and getting new information. Dawn was a couple of hours away, and

Alexander couldn't help but wonder if that was a good sign or not. What the fuck could Cooper want with Sawyer?

His phone began ringing again, and Alexander didn't bother to look at the caller ID, assuming it was his sister once again.

"Hello, sis. Have you found new information?" Alexander asked as he flipped to the speaker once again.

A male voice came on the line surprising everyone in the room. "Sawyer is being held at the Rock-a-Hoola Waterpark in Newberry Springs." Then the line went dead. What the hell?

Alexander looked down at the call display to see if the caller had blocked his identity. As it turned out, he hadn't. "It says, 'Trey Stoneham.'"

The room burst into a hive of activity as calls and plans were made, and the local authorities contacted. Alexander walked up to Miguel, who didn't seem surprised.

"I'm coming along."

"Of course, you are, but stay in the back until the place is cleared."

"Understood." There was no way he'd wait here. Sawyer might need him.

We're coming, baby.

***

Sawyer made it to the car and waited roughly ten minutes before hiding the keys on the tire and heading back down to the waterpark. He couldn't leave Trey behind.

Slowly he weaved his way from one building to another, keeping his eyes and ears open. As he got closer to his original location, Sawyer could hear people talking, so he slowed down and tried to hear what was being said.

"Where is he?" That was the voice of his kidnapper.

"He was gone when I got here," Trey's voice answered. The guy had Trey.

Then a second voice began talking. "Why don't you give the man a little incentive to jog his memory?" Sawyer knew that voice as well, Cooper. The fucker had had him followed and kidnapped. He had to be crazy.

Suddenly a gunshot broke the silence of the early morning along with Trey's cry. Sawyer knew what he had to do, and he hoped the people he loved forgave him for risking his life like this.

Sawyer made his way around the arcade and back to the initial hole Trey had cut out for his escape. He peeked in to see if he could tell where the three men were standing. The front door to the arcade was open, and he caught a glimpse of feet outside in front of the arcade.

"Tell me where Sawyer is," Cooper insisted.

"Fuck you," Trey spat. His voice echoed the pain he was suffering. "He's long gone. If I'd known what you were up to, I would have never agreed. I would have turned you over to the cops."

"What a waste," Cooper growled. "We'll find Sawyer. Finish him."

Sawyer hurried around the side of the building and came around the corner behind his tall kidnapper. As Marian had taught him over the past weeks, Sawyer let the blade Trey had given him fly with the flick of the wrist. Landing squarely in the middle of Trey's would-be killer's back. The guy fell to the ground, followed by Trey, who appeared to be unconscious. A large patch of blood stained the right side of his chest.

Cooper's shocked expression gave Sawyer only a moment's satisfaction before the asshole pulled out his gun from his jacket.

"Hello, Sawyer," Cooper sneered. "You should have run when you have the chance." Cooper wasn't looking so good. The dark patches under his eyes were black, and his red eyes seemed to be glassed over. Sawyer didn't know what Cooper was on, but he guessed the man's money would give him access to about any drug he wanted.

"I'm not a coward like you sending out others to do your work. If you wanted me, you should have grown some balls and done it yourself. What the hell do you want anyway?"

"What do I want? I thought that would be obvious. My life back that you stole from me."

Sawyer wasn't sure what to make of that statement. "I have nothing that you owned."

"Yes, you do. Alexander was mine."

"Alexander isn't an object."

"We used to take time off, and I'd apologize until he took me back, but not this time. You had to ruin our relationship."

"What relationship? By the sounds of it, you two hadn't been in a relationship for six months before Alexander broke up with you after finding another man's dick up your ass." Sawyer knew he was pushing his luck, but if Cooper wanted to kill him, it didn't matter what Sawyer said, so it might as well be the truth.

"Enough," Cooper yelled, and spittle flew from his chapped lips. "With you gone, everything goes back to normal."

"You think by killing me, you'll get Alexander back? You're crazy."

"Shut up," Cooper growled while punching the barrel of his gun into the air toward Sawyer. "It's time for you to die, and don't worry about your brother. I have plans for him."

"Fuck you. Stay away from Bobby."

Cooper smiled wide, creeping Sawyer out even further because his gums were bleeding. What the hell did he take?

"Goodbye, Sawyer," he said as he raised the gun to Sawyer's chest.

Sawyer closed his eyes and waited for the shot. Would he even hear it or be dead instantly? Moments later, he got his answer. He heard the shot, but Sawyer wasn't in any pain. He searched his body and found nothing wrong. His eyes flew open to find Cooper lying on the ground beside his hired kidnapper. Trey was wobbling on his elbow, barely able to hold the gun in his hand.

Sawyer snapped back to reality and went to Trey to help him. The gun clattered to the ground as Trey laid flat on his back. Sawyer took off his t-shirt and pressed it against Trey's chest wound. Sawyer could hear sirens getting louder and knew help was on the way.

"Hang in there, Trey, not much longer," he said desperately, hoping he was right.

Trey's hand dug into his left pocket as if he were searching for something. When he found what he'd wanted, Trey held it out to Sawyer.

"Take this," he said before he began coughing.

Sawyer could see the flashing lights headed their way. "What is it?" he asked while taking the piece of paper from Trey's shaking hand.

"People I take care of," Trey said weakly. "If I die, please help them."

Sawyer opened the piece of paper, and inside was a group photo and an address. The people in the picture varied in age from infant to white hair, and they all were smiling. He was about to ask who they were, but Trey was unconscious.

"I promise to find them and help if I can."

Cruisers streamed into the old waterpark, and there was an ambulance among them. Paramedics took over and soon had Trey on a stretcher and heading to the nearest trauma center. Sawyer clutched at the blanket an officer had given him as he repeated the events of the last twelve hours.

The coroner came to collect Cooper and his lackey, Sawyer never did catch his name, as a new group of cruisers pulled into the waterpark. Even from this far away, Sawyer could make out Alexander leaping from the lead car. When their eyes met, everything Sawyer had been through finally hit home, and tears began flowing. Alexander's image blurred as tears filled Sawyer's eyes, but he knew those arms when they wrapped around him.

"I've got you, baby. Everything's going to be okay."

Alexander's calming words felt like a balm to Sawyer's ravaged soul, and there was no other place he wanted to be.

***

It was Christmas Eve, and Sawyer was moments away from the end of his shift. They'd closed early so the staff could celebrate with their families. Marian had thought he was crazy for wanting to go back to work so fast after his kidnapping, but he needed the distraction.

Trey was recovering in the hospital, and as for the people he'd asked Sawyer to look after, Trey said it wouldn't be necessary because he'd lived. That didn't mean Sawyer wasn't curious about who the people were, but he respected Trey's privacy.

As for his part, Trey wouldn't accept that he wasn't at fault even though he'd been cleared of wrongdoing. In fact, Trey had an up-to-date PI License and a permit for the gun he'd been carrying.

Alexander had been by Sawyer's side day and night unless he was working in the kitchen, in which case Alexander would come back and check on Sawyer. Tonight, he was away from The Gates picking his sister up from the airport.

Sawyer stacked the last of the clean dishes and threw all his wet dishcloths in the laundry bucket. He took one last look around his work area to make sure it was spotless and then removed his apron.

He ran into Marian, Saint, and Max on his way through the restaurant's dining room.

"Merry Christmas, Sawyer, and this is for you," Saint said as he handed him an envelope. "A little gift to show you how much we appreciate your hard work around here.

"Thank you, sir," Sawyer said as he looked down at the thick envelope. He'd never gotten a Christmas bonus before.

"Have a wonderful night," Marian said, and the three carried on into the kitchen to continue handing out envelopes.

Sawyer made his way to the private elevators and pressed the button to take him home to the third floor. His front door wasn't far from the elevator, so within seconds he was sliding his keycard over the pad.

When he opened the door, the condo wasn't the same as when Sawyer had left it. More garland and lights were strung over every wall, and Christmas songs played in the background. He took a few steps in and looked into the living room to find a live Christmas tree covered in lights and surrounded by presents.

Sawyer was beginning to wonder where everyone was when a cheer broke out, and his family began streaming out of the master bedroom where they'd been hiding. Alexander, Bobby, Janice, Jillian, and Oscar gathered in the living room in front of Sawyer.

"Merry Christmas, baby," Alexander said as he came over and hugged Sawyer.

"What'd ya think, bro? And the tree is real. Can you smell the pine?" Bobby asked, his face lit up as he looked at the tree.

"It's so beautiful. Thank you all for this amazing surprise."

Sawyer hugged his brother tight. "Merry Christmas, Bobby."

"Merry Christmas, Sawyer."

# Epilogue

*Ten months later*

Sawyer looked up from his laptop and out the window from their new home at 1100 Wilshire Boulevard. The view from the twenty-fourth floor was spectacular. The sun's rays flooded in while the bright blue sky remained vast and cloudless. They'd been able to score a corner condo doubling that phenomenal view. It seemed, the three of them had hit a patch of good luck.

Buildings tall and short surrounded them as far as the eye could see and fading into the horizon. At night, the surrounding buildings, along with the never-ending crush of traffic, lit the freeway like a snake slithering through a jungle.

They lived closer to the Gates than Alexander's previous building, which they both appreciated. They could have purchased a condo at The Gates, but agreed they needed a work/life separation.

"Aren't you supposed to be studying?" Bobby asked as he rolled into the spacious living room. Another reason he, Alex, and Bobby had chosen this location was the open floor plan, and the ease his brother could move his wheelchair around.

"I was," Sawyer said. He'd been reading over the notes he'd taken during a recent online lecture. "Now, I'm taking a break."

Cal State Fullerton had honored Sawyer's scholarship, taking into account the events that'd stopped him from pursuing his degree. He was attending online classes and was maintaining a 3.75 GPA.

"You'd better be after forcing me to go to school," Bobby grumbled.

"Don't give me that shit," Sawyer huffed. "You love your classes and hanging out with friends. You're eighteen and ready for new challenges."

Bobby went to school three days a week and had learned new skills and had regained his zest for life. They'd held his eighteenth birthday party at The Gates and everyone had been invited. Sawyer remembered waking up that morning feeling like he'd won the lottery. They made it. Bobby was an adult. No one nowhere could ever take Bobby from him.

"That reminds me, Finn and Joey are coming by after dinner to hang out and play some games."

"Great," Sawyer said. "Will, you and your friends be raiding the pantry again?" The amount of junk food those three could put away in a single night of gaming was unbelievable.

"Count on it, bro."

"Shit." With the open place, Alexander's voice carried from the kitchen along with a heavenly smell.

Sawyer closed his laptop and went to have a look at what Alexander was cooking. Today, as they had every Sunday morning since they began their lives together, they'd taken their weekly trip to the zoo. Aside from seeing their usual friends, they spent time at the new California condor facility's construction site, which was going to be twice the old ones size. Thanks to a generous donation made in their parent's memory from his boyfriend and the Larsen Foundation.

"You okay?" Sawyer asked as he neared the breakfast bar. Alexander had—not without a whole lot of angst about giving up a tiny bit of control of his kitchen—left the Sunday morning and afternoon prep in the hands of his capable sous chef to give them some family time.

Three ribeye steaks sizzling away on the indoor grill as he stirred pearl couscous while writing on a nearby pad of paper.

"Fine."

"How's it coming?" Bobby asked.

Alexander looked up and smiled wide. Sawyer loved that. "Lunch or the notes?"

"Either. Both," Bobby answered for Sawyer, who sat back in one of the counter's chairs.

At Bobby's urging, Alexander had agreed to write a cookbook with Bobby's help. It wasn't quite what you might expect from a Michelin Star chef. Gone were the froufrou spices from some monastery on the top of a mountain, and the small appliances that required a degree in engineering to operate.

The book would be the simple, back to basics method of preparing meals, with a kick. Recipes that rocked without the hours of time investment and cost that not everyone could afford.

Alexander wrote down his recipes from memory, the way he'd cooked them in the high-end restaurants where he'd worked, then he and Bobby would review them. Alexander found ways to make them easier and less expensive to prepare.

Sawyer wasn't so sure about their partnership, but in the end, Bobby spoke for the "average" home cook. It seemed, he was a sponge, and had soaked up a lot of information watching YouTube, and the Food Network.

They'd agreed, all the proceeds from the book's sales would go to organizations feeding the homeless, one of which was Finn's food delivery service for the people on Skid Row.

"Food's almost ready," he answered his attention on his food. He looked up and smiled. "Hi. How's studying going?"

"Good. I'll go over it again tonight to make sure I'm ready for tomorrow's test."

"I'm so proud of you." Alexander kissed his cheeks before letting him go and returning to his food.

Their lives had melded together so seamlessly sometimes it scared Sawyer. Other than his brother and parents, he'd never felt such a connection and worried that at any time, he'd wake up back in his recliner in their one-bedroom apartment. He still had his father's recliner, but it had taken up residence in his office. There'd be no more sleeping on it.

"I put out the napkins. Could you set the table?" Alexander asked.

"You got it," Sawyer replied. He walked over to the buffet sitting along the wall in the dining room with Bobby right behind him.

Sawyer dug out three plates and set them on Bobby's lap along with the forks and knives. His brother followed him as Sawyer took a plate and corresponding utensils from his lap and placed them on the table beside the napkins Alexander had already set out.

"Seriously, bro," Bobby laughed. "You didn't even flatten out the napkin in front of your spot."

Sawyer backed up and pushed his palm against it, and it wouldn't flatten. What the hell? He picked up the napkin and searched through the folds until he found the cause.

138

The breath was sucked out of his lungs as the sun gleamed off the gold band. Three large inset diamonds flashed as his mind raced. He turned from the table to find Alexander kneeling behind him.

Shit. Sawyer was going to pass out.

Alexander grabbed hold of his hands before he dropped the ring. Bobby seemed to have disappeared.

"My life has become full and robust in ways I could never have imagined before you let me in. You are the ingredient that makes me whole. I never want to be without you. I love you. Will you marry me?"

"I'm not dreaming, right?" Sawyer had to ask.

Alexander's wide smile was all the confirmation Sawyer needed before he threw himself into his lover's arms.

"Of course I'll marry you."

Everything after that was a blur. They ate lunch. There was a cake that Alexander and Bobby had kept hidden to celebrate the engagement, along with champagne.

After lunch, Alexander had to go to work, but when he crawled into bed late that night, he woke Sawyer in the most delicious way, and later he fell back asleep ensconced in Alexander's arms.

For years, Sawyer thought fate had dealt him and Bobby a crappy hand and that was all they'd ever get. With Alexander's patience and love, Sawyer was beginning to accept the gifts he'd been given and be grateful for having possibilities again.

That was a recipe for a happy life.

## *SAINT*

The slam of his office door shook the dust from the old paintings still clinging to the walls of plaster, and the sound of breaking glass confirmed one had lost its battle to hold on. Saint threw yet another folder into his recycling bin before leaning back into his chair and looking up at the stained ceiling. Was he asking too much?

"You send another one packing, boss?" Larry asked as he stuck his head in through the now opened door.

"There has to be one contractor out there who sees my vision for this dump," Saint groaned. "They want to gut everything."

Larry walked all the way in and sat on one of the high-back, upholstered chairs from the lounge area. Saint didn't even know the guy's last name, but that hadn't mattered when he'd found Larry sleeping in the corner of his building's entryway. Larry had needed help and so had Saint. It worked out for both of them. At first, Saint had kept an eye on the young homeless man as he helped around the building, but after two months, Saint had learned to relax a bit. If Larry had intended to steal from him, he would have done it by now.

Saint looked down at his leather-covered hands. The black, fingerless gloves were designed to support and protect his still-healing hands from the wounds that had changed everything. Larry had been indispensable, so Saint had provided him with a room of his own in the back of the building as well as a cash allowance of sorts. Considering Saint paid for all the expenses and food, Larry was pocketing enough to take care of himself without resorting to other means.

"They can't gut what makes this old building unique. My grandpa used to say there was too much conformity in the world," Larry answered as he wiped his sweaty, dust-covered face, leaving one clean streak down the side. Saint wasn't sure where Larry had been raised, but his accent suggested the mid-west.

"Damn straight," Saint agreed before standing with a soft hiss of pain.

"Your side hurting again?" Larry asked.

There had been three bullets that day. One for each hand and a third through his stomach, tearing a hole in his small intestines that had required over ten hours of surgery to repair.

"It's not bad." Short and to the point, Saint refused to talk about his injuries. The quicker he healed, the faster he could put that chapter in his life to rest once and for all.

Larry followed him out of the office Saint had created from the old storage room behind the solid oak bar. He had been surprised no one had ripped it out considering it looked like it dated back to the building's beginnings. The wood was carved into various palm leaf shapes and covered an entire wall complete with mirrors. There was no way in hell he'd allow someone to destroy it, which was one of the many stupid things the last contractor had suggested.

Saint had to hand it to Larry—the man worked hard. "This room looks so much better without all the debris and broken furniture. Were you able to find room in the dumpster out back?"

"Yep, it's all ready for pickup. No wasted space."

"Good job. Are you getting hungry?" Saint asked as he looked down at his watch and discovered it was already early evening. Another day gone and nothing to show for it. Why was finding a general contractor such a pain in the ass? It wasn't as if he was asking for the Taj Mahal to be rebuilt.

"I can keep going, boss."

"That's not what I asked."

Larry looked down at his shoes before mumbling, "I could eat."

Saint knew the young man was doing everything in his power not to be a bother. Sometimes it seemed as though Larry would make himself as small as possible to avoid attention. Saint had been working on the young man's confidence, which seemed ironic considering he'd lost his own.

"You need to tell me the truth when I ask you questions. It's the only way this arrangement is going to work. If I lose track of time, you are free to tell me it's past supper and that you're hungry. At least until we can work a small kitchen in here somewhere so you can make whatever you want whenever. Take a shower and we'll figure out something to eat," Saint instructed, bringing a smile to Larry's face before he took off to his room.

Saint had thought to add more to the common space when they'd cleared out the back, or hub, as they began calling it. Their efforts had yielded a space that included a television, couch, his easy chair, a small dining table set, a coffee table, microwave, electric coffeepot, and a small bar fridge.

Looking around, he wished he had more to show for two months' worth of work, but it wasn't as if he had much else to do. Sure, he could have stayed in a comfortable hotel while working out the basics of his design concept, but if he was starting a new life, he needed to jump in with both feet.

The buzzer for the front door sounded—another new addition— and Saint changed direction and headed toward the thick wooden doors. He'd hired the Sentinel crew to install a security system in the building. It was worth the small fortune he'd paid for the peace of mind. While a lot of DTLA had been or was in the process of being renovated, there were as many places that were derelict and some were hard-core dangerous. Saint had vowed never to be caught unaware again.

He looked at the monitor embedded into the wall a few feet from the front doors, checking to see who was out there. He flipped the locks and walked out into the waning sunlight. The warm air hit him and he shook his head. He didn't think he'd ever get used to LA's climate. Early spring back in New York City would hold the possibility of one last grand snowstorm or two, typically after everyone had removed their snow tires, making traffic worse than usual.

Saint walked the ten feet to the imposing gothic wrought-iron gate that enclosed the front vestibule area of the building. He'd had the gates fixed the day after he'd found Larry sleeping in the entryway. A courier was waiting for him, but instead of opening the nine-foot gate, he simply held out his hand for the man to place the envelope in it.

"Dr. Francis Jeffrey?" The busy street noise and mass of people moving along the sidewalks was almost deafening, and Saint quirked a brow at the kid. He asked the question again and Saint nodded. He was no longer a surgeon and wanted people to address him as mister, but this kid wouldn't know that.

The kid handed a handheld device through the gate's bars. "Sign here," he said in a bored monotone voice. Saint hated this part. Carefully, he took the stylus from the courier and wrapped his fingers as far as he could around the plastic. No matter how hard he tried, he could only make his index finger reach his thumb and scribbled something illegible on the digital pad. When he went to hand back the device, the expression on the kid's face wasn't surprising. Saint growled and shoved the pad in the guy's hands, took the white envelope, and stormed inside before relocking the door.

He wondered if one day it would get better when he saw the shock and pity in their eyes. If the stabbing pain ripping through his heart would ease over time.

"You should have let me get that for you, boss," Larry said as he came running to the front doors. His hair was still damp but at least he was dressed. All Saint needed was a twenty-something traipsing around in a towel.

He treated Larry as he would his brother Johnny, and made that clear after the one and only time the man had made a pass at him. Saint knew it had to have been tough on the street, and Larry probably assumed there would be a price for Saint's kindness. It took some reinforcing, but it seemed Larry believed Saint wanted nothing more than an honest day's work for Larry's efforts. The fact that he felt responsible for Larry and treated him like Johnny, the brother he'd protected by staying away, was a matter Saint didn't want to look at too closely.

# ABOUT THE AUTHOR

M. Tasia is a M/M romance author who lives in Ontario, Canada. She's is a dedicated people watcher, lover of romance novels, 80's rock, and happily-ever-afters (once the MCs are put through their paces, of course), who grew up with a love of reading. She's a firm believer that everyone deserves to have love, excitement, and crazy hot romance in their lives. Love should be celebrated and shared.

### Connect with M.:
mtasiabooks.com
facebook.com/mtasiabooks
twitter.com/mtasiaauthor
instagram.com/m.tasia.author/

**www.BOROUGHSPUBLISHINGGROUP.com**

If you enjoyed this book, please write a review. Our authors appreciate the feedback, and it helps future readers find books they love. We welcome your comments and invite you to send them to info@boroughspublishinggroup.com. Follow us on Facebook, Twitter and Instagram, and be sure to sign up for our newsletter for surprises and new releases from your favorite authors.

Are you an aspiring writer? Check out www.boroughspublishinggroup.com/submit and see if we can help you make your dreams come true.

www.ingramcontent.com/pod-product-compliance
Lightning Source LLC
Chambersburg PA
CBHW071308130626
46556CB00004B/1521